No one knows what they're made of until they're broken. At the tender age of twenty-two, Hope Ali has finally joined the organization of her dreams, the Agency, an elite group of attorneys who go undercover to right wrongs the law can't. The requirements are stringent, the training exhausting.

After seeking asylum in the United States when she was sixteen, Hope and her father, Sheikh Harun Ali, settled in a quiet Wisconsin town, hiding from those who had placed a price on their heads. Still, she excelled, finishing her university and law school education by the time she was twenty-one.

Now, after breezing through the Agency training program, Hope appears to be indestructible—until she is assigned a simple task during the rescue of an author among the disappeared in the UAE. The task? To distract the woman's captors until she can be spirited out of the country.

Unfortunately, a member of MISix has other plans. In an attempt to disrupt the Agency's mission, she tips off one of Hope's enemies, alerting them to her location. Hope manages to lead the author's captors on a merry dance, freeing others to rescue her, until she is unexpectedly confronted with a violent angry mob intent on harm.

She is left bloody and broken. No one knows whether Hope's body or her mind will heal. Suddenly Hope is no longer just her name. It is also the one thing she must embrace to find her new normal.

Hope
Copyright © 2019 Seelie Kay
ISBN: 978-1-4874-2675-0
Cover art by Martine Jardin

Published by eXtasy Books Inc or
Devine Destinies, an imprint of eXtasy Books Inc

Look for us online at:
www.eXtasybooks.com or www.devinedestinies.com

HOPE
FEISTY LAWYERS BOOK 4

BY

SEELIE KAY

DEDICATION

To everyone who has ever been broken and managed to heal, finding hope.

CHAPTER ONE: PIPSQUEAK

Agent Dianna Murphy glared at the stopwatch she held in her hand.

"Dammit," she murmured into her Bluetooth. "She broke the speed record again, Boyd. We need to shake things up. Shake *her* up. Our obstacles are simply too easy for her. Hope is too light on her feet. She flies through the course as if she's sprouted wings.

"But when she comes up against some three-hundred-pound gorilla, twice her height and three times her weight, she's gonna have a fight on her hands. We aren't doing her any favors by making this too easy. She needs a challenge. A *big* challenge."

Boyd muttered an obscenity. "You're right, of course. What do you suggest?"

"We need a tougher course, something so hard it leaves her dirty, exhausted, and pissed. Something she can't conquer in a single try. Something that forces her to utilize every ounce of her training. I want to see her cry in frustration, sulk in despair. We can't mess with this course, not when others are using it, but we can create something of our own."

"And what if she complains? Makes that age-old cry of gender discrimination?"

Dianna chuckled. "That's not Hope's way. The Ali's have taught her well. She's tougher than anyone on this base. Hell, she's even better trained in self-defense than anyone on this base. And smarter, so much smarter. But she's book smart, not street smart. We have to challenge her to overcome the

1

deficits she does have in the real world—her size, her strength, her lack of cynicism."

Boyd groaned. "I'm so glad you're training her. Most of the guys around here are afraid of her. She's so sneaky, she's lethal. She took every guy to the mat in the self-defense class, not because she was bigger or stronger, but because she's smart. Those bodyguards she had taught her every single dirty trick. Any way you look at it, she's going to be a superstar."

Dianna grunted. "Well, a dead superstar is still dead. It's my job to make sure she survives, no matter the situation." She flipped through the pages on her clipboard. "I was given information on a course that is more challenging, but it's been sitting in mothballs. No one has used it for a few years. Something called *The Ballbuster*."

Boyd remained silent for a moment. "Damn, Dianna. Only a few people have gotten through that course successfully, and your husband, Anders, was one of them. Even he had to run it a few times before he mastered it. That thing is brutal. What if Hope fails? What if she breaks?"

"This is Hope Ali we're talking about. At the ripe old age of twenty-two, the best recruit the Agency has ever had. She will not break. And if she fails, she will pick herself up and keep on trying. I guarantee it."

"God, I am so glad you're her trainer. When that kid gets pissed, no one wants to be in her line of fire."

Dianna laughed. "Speaking of which, how'd she do with the assault weapons? Were they too heavy for her?"

Boyd snickered. "Of course they were. She could barely pick one up, but that didn't stop her. She still managed to best everyone else in her class. Grabbed a bale of hay, dragged the gun over, and used the hay for arm support. Figured out how to handle the blowback and just started shooting. Half the men walked away looking like they had been forced to feast on their balls for breakfast. Some of them were actually tossed on their asses from the recoil action. Not Hope Ali. She punched the bull's eye repeatedly and did a dainty little happy dance. At least we don't have to worry about her hooking up with any of the other recruits. They've all been emasculated."

"Good. She doesn't need the distraction."

"Well, except for Agent Jeffries, that is. Man has it bad, though he'll never admit it. He stares at her with those sad puppy dog eyes. Can't take his eyes off her. She doesn't even notice. Practically ignores him. Poor guy."

"Do I need to speak with Jeffries?"

"His superiors are well aware of his interest. If he takes it any further, all of her protectors are ready to swoop in and bat him away."

Dianna laughed. "That's what happens when you grow up surrounded by the Agency. You get your own built-in cockblocking squad, whether you want it or not."

Hope Ali stormed into her dorm room and threw herself down on the narrow twin bed that awaited her. She groaned, rolled over, and stared up at the ceiling. "Dammit, dammit, dammit," she cursed. "This is not fair. I passed all of their damn tests. What more do they want?"

Cate Creighton, her assigned Agency mentor and roommate, rolled over and pushed her long blonde hair out of her big blue eyes. She sighed dramatically. "They want you to prove that you can best the men and women you're going to meet out in the field. Face it, Hope. In here, you're mighty. But that really doesn't prove anything.

"When you're hunkered down in Russia or the Middle East, confronted by four-hundred-pound enforcers who can crush you with their boot, you're going to be in trouble unless you can get past them. To the enemy, you're going to be a butterfly waiting to be scooped up in a net. You need to be faster, smarter, more lethal than your opponents. It's the Agency's job to make sure you're prepared—for anything. They put me through hell, too, but I survived. And so will you."

Hope scowled. "You've only got a few inches on me, yet you breezed right through training. We have similar backgrounds. Both of us grew up with bodyguards and excessive defense training because of who our parents are. Why is this so much easier for you?"

Cate shrugged. "We don't have the same challenges. I've got five inches and probably twenty or thirty pounds on you, and I know how to use it. Besides, we're being trained for different roles. I'll always be the honey pot, the seductress. I need to be more subtle in how I attack and defend myself. You don't. Most times, I'll be one-on-one with most of my targets. And as I have proved, in the heat of the moment, I am quite capable of eliminating them if need be. There's little chance that I will ever have to face an armed man or an angry mob. You can't make the same claim."

Two years prior, working undercover for her mother, Lydia Creighton, the U.S. Ambassador to the U.N., Cate had infiltrated the Latin American compound of the notorious religious cult, God's Delight. Her job had been to determine whether cult members were being used as slave labor to harvest and manufacture heroin. Unbeknownst to her, Dianna Murphy and her husband, Agent Anders Mark, were also working undercover to ascertain how the cult was recruiting American college students and whether those students were being held against their will.

Cate, who had garnered the attention of the cult's leader and used that attraction to solicit information, had emerged unscathed. Dianna, however, had been poisoned, and without Cate's intervention, could have lost her life. Shortly thereafter, Cate had been asked to join the Agency. Dianna, however, had removed herself from the field and joined the training division.

"And second of all, you're being trained to be invisible. Because of your age and size, you have to ability to move in and out of situations unnoticed. However, that doesn't mean you won't get caught. If you do, you'll have to rely on your instincts to survive. That's what they're trying to teach you, Hope. How to react without thinking, to ensure you survive. A moment's pause, a second of indecision, could kill you."

Cate sat up and began to pull on her cross-trainers. "I have been trained practically since birth how to hone my instincts. I can read people like a book and know how they're going to react even before they do. My life has been filled with parties with diplomats and world leaders. I've met the best and the worst. I can smell deceit. I can sense evil. You didn't have that experience. For your safety, your father had to keep you out of the public eye. So you haven't had an opportunity to develop street smarts. That's what they're trying to give you now, street smarts. You're not there yet, but you will be." Cate smiled. "And once you can read people, you and I are going to head to Vegas and slay some poor suckers in a few poker tournaments. You know, the ones with all the hotshot actors? We'll glam up, make them think we're nothing but fluff, and clean their clocks. We'll be able to read all of their tells. They'll be begging for mercy." Cate sighed happily.

Hope groaned. "And I'll be drinking water, despite the free alcohol. I still haven't recovered from my twenty-first birthday party, when you and everyone else thought it would be fun to teach me drinking games. I felt like crap for two weeks afterward."

Cate snorted. "That's when we realized you'd never be able to drink a thug under the table. You, my dear, need to play a whole different ballgame." She finished tying her shoes and stood. "Come on, time to check out tonight's protein-packed fare. I never thought I would say this, but I am so sick of fish, beef, and chicken that I would welcome a little tofu and spirulina. I'm starting to bulk up like a tackle for the Green Bay Packers."

Hope giggled. "There *is* something to be said for being able to roll over and crush your prey."

Cate's eyes widened. She picked up her pillow and whipped it toward Hope's head. "Watch it, *pipsqueak*. The next person I roll over could be you."

Hope grabbed the pillow and tossed it back. "Ah, but you can bet Agent Jeffries will be there to rescue me." Her eyes narrowed. "Don't you think calling me *pipsqueak* is just a little disrespectful? All of you call me that, and I'm starting to feel insulted. It was okay when I was a teenager, but now . . ."

Cate waved her off. "Accept it for what it is, a term of affection. Almost every agent you work with knew you as a kid. They adore you. Calling you *pipsqueak* isn't an insult, it a way of reminding you of their long-term bond with you." Cate frowned. "If you really hate it, we'll stop. But there are much worse nicknames out there. *Killer. The Assassin. Wonder Woman.*"

Hope shrugged. "At least those nicknames have nothing to do with my age or my size. I'm not some mini-me. I am a full-grown adult who just happens to be height-challenged. Though sometimes, I feel like everyone is expecting me to fail because of it."

Cate laughed. "Actually, it's just the opposite. They're impressed by your skills. You're killing it, girl, and don't you forget it." She grinned. "Now about Agent Jeffries. Despite that aloof, tall, dark, and handsome thing he's got going on, he's practically velcroed to your ass. And not in a good way. If he becomes your partner, he may be more interested in—"

Hope slapped her hands over her ears. "Ugh. No more. That's a visual I don't need."

Cate smiled sweetly. "Then you'd better bring a towel . . . to wipe up the drool. Dude's got it baaaaaaad."

Agent Thomas Jeffries waited impatiently in the cafeteria for the woman who consumed his every waking thought, Hope Ali. At age twenty-five, he was no longer a hormone-driven teenager. No, he was a fully-trained covert operative who had escaped scores of life-threatening situations, besting the bad guys and tossing them into cells. Yet one teeny tiny woman with long thick, silky black hair and big, brown soulful eyes had reduced him to a sniveling puddle of need. When those full, ruby red lips opened and released those dulcet British tones, his knees grew weak and his cock hard. Even when she was insulting him.

Sure, Hope Ali was a handful. But he wanted her to be *his* handful. As in his hands. As . . .

Dammit, he had it bad for that sweet little princess. Oh, she was polite enough. She smiled when they met. She even deigned to engage him in conversation. But nothing more. She treated him like all the other guys and that had to stop. His grandfather had taught him that seduction took time and only then was surrender unconditionally sweet. So he would patiently weave his spell. He would woo Hope. Romance her. Seduce her. And once he captured her heart, mind, and soul, he would envelop her in unwavering bliss.

Until she kicked him in the balls, cackled, and danced away.

Tom chuckled to himself. That was the challenge of Hope Ali. She was a vision of loveliness, as angelic as they came. Until she opened her mouth or unleashed a lethal kick. Then she was a warrior, a woman on a mission. She gave a whole new meaning to the term *warrior princess.*

He smiled at Hope when she appeared before him. She blushed, then rushed into the food line, throwing various items onto her tray with abandon. Her roommate, Cate, followed close behind. Cate winked at him and then pointed at Hope, rolling her eyes. Relief filled him. At least Cate appeared to be on his side. She was a great ally.

Tom's attention was drawn to the sound of tiny feet running into the cafeteria. A little voice yelled, "Hope! Hope! Over here! I missed you!" He watched with amusement as a tow-headed boy about four ran toward Hope and wrapped his arms around her waist while she struggled to balance her tray. Tom strode toward her and took the tray out of her hands. "Woah, looks like you have your hands full."

The little boy giggled. "Hope's my girlfriend," he said. "We gonna get married someday."

Hope grinned and peeked up at Tom through thick black lashes. "What's eighteen years when it's true love?" She patted the boy's head and then squatted down to kiss his cheek. "Ethan, do your parents know where you are?"

A loud laugh boomed from the entrance to the cafeteria. Cade Matthews, Agent-in-Charge, walked in with his wife, former Agent and now law professor Janet MacLachlan. A tiny little girl, with the same light blonde hair and big blue eyes of her mother, shyly hugged Janet's leg. The child's gaze swept the cafeteria, then locked onto Hope. She ran toward her, squealing with delight. "Opey!" she yelled as she launched herself at Hope, knocking the little boy aside.

Hope swept the girl into her arms and laughed. "Chloe! Oh, how I've missed you." She set the little girl on the floor and took both children's hands. "My mighty misfits, back together again." She grinned happily.

Tom smiled as he watched the boy and girl shower Hope with affection. He cleared his throat and gestured toward the food tray he still held. "Um, what do you want me to do with this?"

Cade laughed and walked over to him. "Just put it down anywhere. My God, Hope. Here only four weeks in, and already you've got a man doing your bidding." He turned and smiled at Tom. "And Agent Jeffries, no less. Good catch. Your father and mother would approve."

Hope stared at Cade and her face paled. "He's not . . . I mean, we're not . . . I barely . . ."

Janet laughed and slapped at her husband. "Oh, cut it out. You've embarrassed them." She smiled at Hope. "However, you and I should talk. Agency relationships, though permitted, are tricky."

Hope's face reddened and she muttered, "But there's nothing going on." She gestured at Tom and said softly, "Just put my tray down anywhere, please. I imagine the Matthews family is joining me for dinner."

Tom nodded, then started to walk away.

Ethan kicked at him and scowled. "Hope's my girlfriend, so you just stay away." He hugged Hope again. "*Forever.*"

Chloe looked at Hope, then at Tom. She grinned. "Wanna be in the wedding!" She began to dance around them. "I can be a pwincess and thow flowers." She clapped her hands with enthusiasm. "Can I, pwease, can I?"

Hope glared at Tom. "See what you started? Now, just take that fine a . . ." Hope blanched. "Oh, just go away." She turned from him and stomped her foot.

Tom smiled and winked at Cate. *Progress.*

CHAPTER TWO: THE BALLBUSTER

Hope stared at the pit full of ice, then gazed at Dianna. "You want me to do what?"

Dianna smiled. "This is your new obstacle course. It's called *The Ballbuster*. Obviously, the other one wasn't challenging enough for you, so I thought we'd try something else." She smirked. "What's the matter, not up to it, Probie?"

Hope scowled. "I thought you were my friend."

"When you're on Agency grounds, I'm your trainer and mentor first. You know that, Hope. My job is to make sure that when in the field, you can overcome every obstacle. Failure isn't an option. Failure could mean death."

Hope snapped, "Don't you think I know that? God, everyone seems duty-bound to remind me of that every damn day. I'm not a child. I know my limits. I know my weaknesses. You don't have to bludgeon me over the head with a cudgel."

Dianna's expression hardened. "Here's the thing, Hope. The second you begin to believe that you can overcome every obstacle put in front of you is the day you should quit. Confidence is one thing. Feeling that you're omniscient is another. Out in the field, fear is what drives you, and it could very well be what saves you. I don't need you taking stupid chances because you think you're *Wonder Woman*, able to thwart every threat. I need you to calmly assess each situation and rationally weigh the risks. You need to know when to walk away. Just as you need to know when a risk is worth taking. You have no real superpowers, woman. And you need to remember that. That's why you're on probation until we're confident you can survive, Probie.

"This job isn't about physical skill. It's about being able to clearly, quickly, and competently analyze the risks. What I see right now is a young woman without fear, willing to take on any roadblock. I need you to recognize your limits and work around them. There is no shame in admitting defeat. And there most definitely is no shame in asking for help. That's why each obstacle has a kill bell. Hit that and the exercise stops."

"And then what," Hope muttered. "I get kicked out?"

"No, then we step in and help. This Agency leaves no man or woman behind, Hope. They proved that to me when I was sent to Bolivia. The minute I sent out the Bat Signal, they began putting together a team to extract me. They saved my life."

The Bat Signal was a GPS driven power cell placed on each agent's back teeth before the commencement of a mission. When an agent got into trouble and required assistance, they bit down on the device and the Agency organized an extraction immediately.

Hope studied the new obstacle course. "Has anyone else run this course successfully?"

"Only four people."

"Any of them women?"

"Yes."

Hope groaned. "Let me guess. Cade, Anders, Janet, and you. All super agents. Agency legends."

Dianna laughed. "Wow. You give me way too much credit. I didn't make it past the first obstacle course. Actually, only one woman has successfully run this course. Cate."

Hope frowned. "No way."

Dianna smirked. "Cate listens well, and she retains everything. She has a photographic memory. Her years of training as an Ambassador's kid enabled her to step into this program and excel. She works hard and does not give up. It took her four tries, but she finally conquered this course."

"No kill bells?"

"Oh, there were plenty of kill bells. But each time she failed, she analyzed the videotapes and figured out what she did wrong. Cate's very analytical. She breaks things down into steps. That's what makes her so good, and that's why she's your roommate. You can learn from her, Hope. Take advantage of her knowledge and experience. She's been out in the real world. She understands people, politics, and power. You have book smarts. Our job is to give you street smarts. Cate can help."

Hope took a deep breath. Cate had been her roommate for a few short months when both attended the University of Wisconsin-Madison. Unbeknownst to Hope, Cate was on assignment. To the outside world, Cate had played a misfit, an entitled trust fund kid who had flunked out of two colleges because of her wild behavior. She pretended to be a promiscuous party animal. And when she had gotten involved with a cult, God's Delight, Hope was prepared to kick her out.

Then Cate traveled to Bolivia with Dianna and Anders for a supposed charitable project. Dianna and Anders had been on assignment. They were supposed to find the location of the God's Delight compound, find the President's goddaughter and, if necessary, extract her as well as determine whether a welfare check was required for any other American citizens living in the compound. Things went sideways when Dianna was poisoned and got deathly ill. When Anders attempted to bring her home, a gunfight had broken out and a number of cult members had been killed or injured.

Hope had later learned that Cate, working undercover for an unknown employer, had been instrumental in getting Dianna out. Then she had disappeared. Hope had not seen her again until her arrival for Agency training.

"Which men finished the course?"

Dianna smiled. "Guess."

"Cade, Anders, and . . ." Hope wrinkled her nose and paused. "Oh my God, do not tell me it was Jeffries!"

Dianna lightly punched her arm. "Okay, I won't. But it was. That guy's in line for great things. He became Anders' partner after I joined the training team. Anders thinks the world of him, and so do I. That guy can think on his feet. He has very good instincts.

"In fact, you should consult with both Cate *and* him. Get some tips on this course."

"How many times did he run this course before he successfully completed it?"

"Three."

Hope scowled. "Then I'll do it in two."

"Oh, I see. So that's how it is, *hmmm*?" Dianna laughed.

Hope narrowed her eyes. "What?"

"Methinks there may be another Agency couple in the making."

Hope shook her head. "Not happening." She wrinkled her nose. "He is so not my type. He's bossy and condescending . . ."

"And gorgeous and determined. The guy does not give up, Hope. Rumor has it he has his sights set on you." Dianna grinned. "He'll just keep at you until he wears you down. And you'll enjoy every single minute."

Hope stormed into the pub on Agency grounds and looked around the room. Her gaze zeroed in on Tom Jeffries. He was playing darts with Cate and several others.

It was time for a showdown. He was messing with her head and her future at the Agency. She was going to put a stop to it.

Hope stomped over to the group. She grabbed a nearly full

bottle of beer out of Tom's hand and took a long swallow. Tom reached for the bottle, but Hope held onto it. She cocked an eyebrow. "What's the matter, Jeffries? Didn't Mommy teach you to share?"

"Sure thing, *princess*. She also taught me some manners. Such as keeping my hands off what's not mine. Stealing someone else's beer is just rude. I thought you were better than that, Hope." He turned and walked away.

Hope's mouth dropped open. "Wait," she squeaked. "I'm sorry, that *was* rude." She hurried over to him. "Let me buy you a beer. I wouldn't want you to catch *girl cooties* or something." *Oh God, why am I apologizing? I wanted him to go away. Just shut up, Hope!*

Tom glared at her. "What is it with you, Hope? One minute you're flirting. The next you're behaving like a stone-cold bitch. I can't tell if you hate me or if you want to get into my pants." He growled. "You'd better make up your mind, because I am almost at the end of my rope. Sooner or later, someone else will catch my attention and I'll move on."

Shit. Fuck. Damn. I came here to chew the guy out. Instead, he's giving me shit. And he's right. I deserve it. Hope blushed. "I'm sorry. You confuse me. I'm not good at dealing with this, whatever this is." She waggled her hand between them. "I came here to tell you to cut it out. Maybe reach an understanding. I don't want the attention. I just want to get through training." She grabbed his hand and pulled him toward the bar. "At least let me buy you a new beer." She peered up at him. "Then maybe we can shoot pool or play darts?" She removed her hand from his. *Odd, his touch was almost . . .*

Tom grunted. "Let me guess. You're a hustler. You'll play the hapless female at pool, then wipe the table with unsuspecting targets. No thanks. My ego can only take so much. Just replace my beer and we'll call it even."

Hope frowned. *Damn. Why does he have to be so difficult?* She walked with him to the bar and ordered his beer. While they waited, she sat on a stool, so her head was almost level with his.

Tom stared at her, a strange expression on his face.

Hope smiled. *God. Agent Jeffries is pretty hot. Cate is right, he is tall, dark, and handsome. And those eyes, those ice blue bedroom eyes.* Her gaze settled on his lips. *His lips are just smoking. So kissable. I really, really want to . . . oh, what the hell . . .* Hope's arm snaked around Tom's neck. His eyes narrowed and filled with suspicion. She pulled him closer and kissed him then pulled back. "I really am sorry." Suddenly feeling shy, she asked, "If I ask you out to dinner, will you say *yes*?"

Tom smirked. "Why don't you ask me and find out? Afraid to take the chance, *princess*?"

The bartender delivered the bottle of beer. Hope handed it to him. "I don't know. You're awfully tall. I'm kind of afraid people will call us *Mutt and Jeff*. Remember? That old cartoon with the short man and the big tall guy?" She huffed. "And stop calling me *princess*. Even though I am one . . . it's . . ." She stared at him. She was having difficulty sounding rational.

Tom laughed. He set down his beer and scooped Hope off the stool and kissed her hard. "I doubt Jeff ever did *this* to Mutt. And yes, you are a *princess*, to me."

Hope wrapped her arms around his neck and kissed him back. *The man knows how to kiss.* She opened her mouth slightly, and he thrust his tongue inside. Hope felt the heat rising in her core. She moaned and allowed his tongue to dance with hers.

Tom's grip on her tightened. His kiss deepened and his tongue began thrusting.

Hope's hand moved to his chest and she gripped his shirt. Her lips moved to his neck. She nipped and sucked.

Tom stroked her hair, then grasped it in his hand and pulled her lips back to his.

A loud cheer went up and they jerked apart. Cate and a few others stood behind them. She grinned. "Thanks, guys. I just won the pool. One hundred bucks." She did a little dance. "I knew you two would be sucking face within a month."

Hope glared at her. "Classy, Cate."

Tom nuzzled her neck. "Let's take this outside." He smirked at Cate. "I imagine the next round is on you." He grinned. "I'll take a raincheck." He pulled Hope more tightly against him, turned, and walked out of the bar.

He carried Hope to his SUV and set her on the ground.

Hope gazed up at him. "Damn. You are tall," she breathed.

Tom grinned. "Well, as you know, it all works out in the bedroom." He lifted her and placed her on the truck's running board. His blue eyes were filled with fire. "And Hope? Yes, I would love to go to dinner with you."

Hope pointed to the first obstacle on *The Ballbuster*, a pool of ice. She scrunched her nose. "I don't even know what this one is called."

Anders Mark laughed. "It's a version of what's called the *Arctic Tunnel*. Basically, it's a pool filled with ice and water. It's layered with webbed plastic, like those things that are used to hold six-packs together, except in one large sheet. You need to find a pathway to the other end. You have to go in headfirst, or your hands and feet will get tangled. However, the way the obstacle is constructed, the webbing moves with the waves you make, often closing off the way to the other side. You need to enter slowly and gently move through it. Most people panic and start thrashing. They never leave the point of entry."

"When will I ever be faced with an ice pit filled with plastic sheets?"

"That's not the point. This obstacle is designed to elicit panic. You can't get through it unless you stay calm and hold your breath. Adjusting to the ice-cold temperature, figuring out how to quickly get to the other side, then emerging within the time limit is tough when your senses are being assaulted by a variety of factors. It's a test of you against the elements."

"Do I at least get to wear a wet suit?"

Anders grinned. "Will you have a wetsuit on when you wind up in a cold river filled with garbage and kelp, desperately trying to find a way out?"

"Well, no."

"Exactly. This obstacle is short. If you keep your wits about you, you should get through it in under a minute. You can hold your breath for three minutes, right?"

Hope nodded.

"Then it should be a piece of cake." Anders gazed at Hope. "Look. If you go in afraid, you'll never get through it. You have a size advantage. Your wake will be smaller than most. Just keep your movements to a minimum and push off from the side to propel yourself through the layers. You'll go in with a rope harness. You are given two minutes to get to the other side. Once the timer goes off, you'll be pulled out unless they see you're making significant progress. They will not let you drown."

"Any tips?"

"Don't think about the cold. Just keep on moving. Blast out of there and run to the next obstacle. That will help warm you up."

Hope nodded. "Noted." She pointed to the next obstacle — a lopsided tunnel built of sheet metal. "What's this?"

Anders chuckled. "Oh, you'll love this one. It's gonna make you cry. This one's called the *Tunnel of Tears*. It's filled with a hot vapor injected with something similar to tear gas. Not only is the place humid as hell, but your eyes will be watering so badly you can barely see. The vapor also makes the metal slippery, so it can be slow going."

Hope sighed. "That sounds awful."

"Actually, if you just give in to the elements, you'll slide right on through. Don't hold your breath or shut your eyes. Instead, use your limited vision to pull yourself through by grabbing the grips on the side and on the floor. Just keep moving. And remember, the vapor is warm, so it rises. Stay as close to the floor as possible, and you won't get overheated."

They moved on to a tall structure with ropes affixed to the top.

"Well, this next obstacle looks familiar. It's a climbing wall."

"Look closely, Hope."

Hope peered up at the wall. "Wait, there are no footings to climb. And the ropes are too short to grapple with."

Anders leaned over and picked up a pole. "First, you have to use this pole to either vault over the top or at least jump high enough to grab the rope and pull yourself over. Then you need to carefully slide down the other side, without falling into the mud pit at the bottom. You need to keep your feet as clean as possible to get through the rest of the course. If you're covered in mud, you won't make it. Slide down this wall and stay out of the mud."

Hope cocked an eyebrow. "Is that legal? I thought wading through the pit was mandatory."

"Ah, young grasshopper. That's an assumption everyone makes. Do as instructed and nothing more."

Hope grinned. "So, I should use the lack of stated rules to win the game?"

"Exactly. You can't avoid any of the obstacles, but only do as instructed. Make no assumptions. Make no additional effort. Your only goal is to complete the course."

Hope walked to the next obstacle. It consisted of three rows of inner tubes laid out in a long path, two tubes high. They appeared to be wired together into one big mass. She frowned. "Well, I can see how the mud could mess this up, but if my feet are dry, this one should be a no-brainer."

"Until this happens." Anders pulled out a remote and the tires began to sway, flip, and deflate, then re-inflate. "You're going to need complete focus and strong reflexes for this one. You won't have time to think about how the tires move. Your body just has to move with them. You have to give in to your reflexes. This is one obstacle that requires you to stop thinking and permit your body to respond instinctively. If you think too hard, you'll screw up."

Hope frowned. "And what if I get stuck under one of those inner tubes?"

Anders pointed to a tree at the end of the course. "Focus on one thing, like that tree over there, and trust your body to move you toward it. I stayed on the tires to the left so I wouldn't get tossed around so much. If you aim for the middle row of tires, there are way too many possibilities. You'll get thrown or stuck. There is no penalty for being thrown onto the ground. You just have to start over. But you are only required to keep one foot on the obstacle at any given time. You can bounce one foot off stable ground to keep or regain your balance. Stick to the right or left row, and you'll do fine."

Hope shook her head and started to giggle. "God, I must have really pissed Dianna off."

"Nope. You challenged her. You made all of your training look too easy, Hope. In essence, you made your bed." He paused. "A word of advice? Perfection is not always a worthy goal. Sometimes, less than perfect gets the job done and is much more expedient."

Hope kicked at some grass. She grumbled, "Is that what everyone thinks? That I'm trying to be perfect?"

"Yup, and now they expect it. You backed your way into a corner. You need to make failure an option, at least in training. You can still pick yourself up and move on. You don't want people to expect perfection. You just want them to trust that you can get the job done. Change your focus. People will respect you more."

A single tear ran down Hope's cheek.

"Oh, God. I made you cry. Shit . . ."

Hope shook her head. "No, you're right. Telling me I don't need to be perfect, that I can make mistakes, is a big relief." She sniffled. "I've heard the comments. I know they call me *Wonder Woman.*" She cleared her throat. "It's just that I've never failed, at anything. It's hard to start now."

"Breathe, pipsqueak. You're human. Let others see that." Anders smirked. "And don't be afraid to fall in love while you're doing so."

Hope's face reddened. "Low blow, Agent Anders."

He smiled. "My God, all Dianna and Cate talk about is you and Agent Jeffries. There's no shame in having someone to lean on, especially someone who has walked your path."

Hope nodded. *Please change the subject. Talking about Agent Jeffries is distracting.* She pointed to the next obstacle, a long, winding collection of bars and wheels with some stairs thrown in at various intervals. "That looks like a jungle gym on steroids."

"Exactly. It's called *Monkey Death.* As in Monkey Bars that can kill. If you're the least bit wet or muddy, you won't be able to hang on. You'll keep falling off. You need to take the time to wipe your hands and feet before latching on."

Hope walked the length of the obstacle and studied it. She stopped and gestured toward the end. "What's this slide thingie at the end?"

"It's a catapult."

Hope stared at it. "As in it picks me up and flings me onto the field?"

"If you put your whole weight on it. If you balance along the sides and distribute your weight evenly, you won't set it off."

Hope stood directly in front of the catapult and studied the field in front of her. It was empty except for a large red slap bell on a fence, about two hundred yards away. "So, if I make it to that bell, I'm done?"

Anders laughed. "Sure, but you still have a line of Ninjas to break through. Most people are so tired at the end of Monkey Death, they drop down without thinking, springing the catapult and landing flat on their backs. The Ninjas are on them before they even get up. You have to keep your wits about you. You want to land on your feet so you're ready to battle the Ninjas."

"Grand."

"You don't have to defeat all the Ninjas. You just have to get past them to ring the bell. I've seen how you fight. This time your crafty and sneaky ways are an advantage. Just give them the slip and ring the bell."

"How many practice runs do I get?"

"None."

"Seriously?"

"Nope. Every try counts. You don't get practice runs in the field, Hope. This is a test of mental and physical agility as well as field readiness. Until you make a successful run within the time allotted, you won't move on."

Hope stomped her foot, her fury mounting. "That's just unfair. You're singling me out. No other woman in my training group has to do this."

Anders' eyes narrowed. "God, Hope, I thought you were above that shit. This has nothing to do with gender and everything to do with survival. Do you honestly think that when you're in the field, *unfriendlies* are going to give you a break because you're a woman?"

Hope flushed. "Well, no."

"Thugs and mugs will think they have an advantage because you're a woman. Your survival depends on proving them wrong."

Chapter Three: The Marriage Contract

Tom waited outside Hope's dormitory, his hands shoved into his pockets.

Hope had adamantly refused to permit him to set foot in the dorm to pick her up. No, the damn woman made him wait outside the doors like a naughty schoolboy. *Geeesh.* He had half a mind to rush inside and march up to her door anyway. Except he didn't have her room number. Tom couldn't wait until this training cycle was done and Hope moved into an apartment. Like a grown-up.

Tom paced impatiently in front of the building. Damn, he was nervous. Finally, he and Hope were going out on an actual date. The mutual attraction was there. The kisses they'd shared the previous week had proved that. Now they needed to discover whether there was something more. Besides lust, that was.

He felt like a teenager in heat. Every encounter with Hope had been an exercise in control. Rubbing out the constant erections that the woman had caused was exhausting. He wanted her in his bed.

Yet he sensed that would not be an easy task. Hope was most definitely not someone who gave off a free unencumbered love vibe. Unlike her friend, Cate, who seemed a little more lighthearted about sexual entanglements, Hope was most definitely a good girl. By all accounts, she didn't sleep around. In fact, she didn't even seem to date. *Heck, she might*

Seelie Kay

even be a virgin.

Suddenly, the anxiety that threatened his stomach took hold. *What the hell am I doing pursuing a virgin?* Crap. He'd lost his virginity at fourteen. He wouldn't even know what to do with a woman who hadn't ever . . .

Hope stepped out of the dorm wearing a pale-yellow sundress and cream-colored stilettos. Her thick black hair was swept off to the side, leaving her slender neck exposed. Her large brown eyes seemed to glow as she caught sight of him. A sweet, sultry smile crossed her gorgeous face.

"Tom," she said softly, her elegant British accent coming out in a purr. "Ready to go?" Her eyes swept his body. "You look nice." She took his hand. "Come on. I've got permission to leave the compound. We can take my car. I have a yearning for slow-roasted ribs." She stopped and looked up at him. Her face took on a quizzical expression. "You do like ribs?"

Tom swallowed. He'd eat okra five thousand ways if it meant he could spend an evening with this woman. He smiled. "Love ribs. Where are we headed?"

"I thought I'd take you to one of the barbecue places I like in Fredericksburg. My version of comfort food." She smiled and rubbed her stomach. "After the day I've had, I need lots of comfort." She flushed. "Oh, I didn't mean *that*. I mean food, *just* food."

Tom laughed. "It's okay, Hope. I get it. Just food and great conversation with a beautiful woman. Even if the food sucks, I still win." He took her hand. "Tell me about this tough day."

"Anders walked me through a second obstacle course today. I believe you know it. *The Ballbuster*? For once, I think my size may work against me." She groaned. "Maybe if I bulk up on protein, I'll be able to conquer it a little more easily." Hope flexed a bicep. "It's either that, or I'm going to have to cheat."

Tom stopped and pulled her into his arms and kissed her gently. "Princess, I am convinced you can do anything. All you have to do is try." He hugged her. "But if you need help, you know where to find me."

Hope's stomach growled loudly and she blushed.

"But first, let's get you fed. Rumor has it you get crabby when you're hungry."

Hope emitted a sigh of satisfaction. It had been the perfect evening. Great food, a hot man, even a perfect glass of fruity red wine. She could get used to this.

She pushed her plate away, smiled, and nodded at the waiter, who took her plate. She daintily blotted her mouth with a wet nap, then wiped her hands. She grinned at Tom. "Best ribs, ever. Right?"

Tom laughed. "I don't know what was better. Watching you devour a rack and a half of ribs, or the ribs themselves."

"My mother thinks I have a tapeworm. She says I eat as much as our bodyguards."

"Your mom's Marianne Benson, right?"

Hope nodded.

He cocked his head. "What's it like growing up with a famous lawyer for a mother?"

Hope took a sip of her wine. "She didn't become my mom until I was sixteen. Before that, it was just me and my dad. My birth mom only lived six days after I was born."

Tom's eyes filled with compassion. "Wow. I'm sorry. So just you and your dad?"

Hope nodded. "Yes. It wasn't always easy. All my brothers were already out of the house. I don't think my dad knew what to do with a little girl. He tried. He was always very loving, but he just had no experience. I had a nanny until I was shipped off to a Swiss boarding school at six. After that, I didn't see much of him because he was so busy. In fact, moving to the United States — despite the fact we were on the run and seeking asylum — has been the best thing that ever happened to me. Sure, at first, we were scared, but once we got settled and my dad married my mom, I felt like I was finally home. Safe. With a real family."

Tom smiled. "So you like living on a farm?"

Hope nodded. "And I loved going to an American high school, being with real kids. Most of the people at boarding school were very wealthy. They'll never have to work a day in their lives. Not a lot of ambition in that group. Just a whole lot of entitlement. Besides, my mom and dad run a cooking school at the farm each summer for disadvantaged and disabled kids. It's a lot of fun. I like that they understand the importance of giving back."

A confused expression crossed Tom's face. "What happened to practicing Law?"

"Oh, they still dabble, usually at the request of the President of the United Nations. But they are rarely on the front lines anymore. They are training others to sue terrorists and terrorist groups to get compensation for the victims of their violence. A few years back, we had a very close brush with death. Some terrorists hijacked a plane and buried it in the cornfield next to my parent's farm, the passengers still on board. Meanwhile, one of the terrorists infiltrated my high school, posing as a star soccer player from Ireland. I'm embarrassed to say he started to pursue me and I almost fell for it."

"Wow, that must have been a real head trip."

"Thankfully, my parents and Cade and Janet figured out what was going on in time. Just as the guy was preparing to shoot up the school, they shut him down. Turns out he planned to use me to get to my parents and kill them."

Tom grabbed her hand. "Jesus, Hope. How old were you?"

"Seventeen. I was a senior in high school." She gazed at Tom. "But that wasn't the worst part. My dad, Cade, Dianna, and Anders found the plane and managed to get all the passengers out alive. My dad and Cade were standing right next to the plane when the terrorists blew it up."

Hope began to choke up and grabbed a glass of water, fighting back tears. "Cade and my dad were in comas for days. We didn't know if they would live. It was the absolute worst thing I have ever been through.

"But it's also the reason I joined the Agency. I witnessed pure evil that day. And I won't let people like that win."

Tom studied her, his fingers stroking hers. "Wow. That explains so much." He gave her a slight smile. "You're kind of a hardass. Despite your size, most of the guys are afraid of you. You're one lethal little bulldog wrapped up in this amazing, smart and sexy package."

Hope cocked an eyebrow. "Is that a compliment?"

Tom kissed her hand, his gaze never leaving hers. "Absolutely."

A short, heavy young man appeared by their table. His dark brown eyes, framed by thick black hair, were filled with disdain. His thin lips curled up into a leering smile. "Why, Amal," he said in a harsh Middle Eastern accent. "We meet again. You really should stop trying to avoid your betrothed. I am starting to think you are trying to nullify our marriage contract."

Hope turned to the speaker and her eyes narrowed. "Rami. What the bloody hell are you doing here?" She scowled. "Following me again? Really, would you get a clue?"

The man, dressed in an expensive-looking suit, stiffened. An expression of arrogance crossed his face. "Really, Amal. I thought you had better manners. So unbecoming for a princess and my future wife." He smiled condescendingly at Tom. "Introduce me to your *friend* . . . or is he your *bodyguard*?"

Hope stood and pushed a finger into Rami's chest. She continued to jab at him, pushing him away from the table and Tom. "You do not speak to me or my friend that way you . . . you arrogant pig." She kept her furious voice low. "If you do not want me to take you down right now, in front of all of these people, some of whom I am sure are already recording this encounter on their phones, I suggest you get the hell out of here. I have a gun with me, and I would love to use it — to shoot your balls off — that is if they aren't already rotting from all the twats you've dipped your wick in."

Rami scowled. "How dare you! Take your hands off me." He pushed her finger away from his chest. "I expect when I get you alone, you will have a much different attitude. A more amenable one."

A tall, muscular man with white-blond hair and piercing blue eyes sidled up behind Rami and grabbed his arm, twisting it behind Rami's back. "Like that's ever going to happen, asshole."

Rami tried to jerk away, but the man held him tightly. Rami turned his head slightly. "Why, Hazelton. I assumed your bodyguard duties had ended once Amal left home." He tried to pull away again. "Let me go, you overgrown ape."

Warren Hazelton had been Hope's bodyguard since she arrived in America. Now, he only protected her when she left the training compound. Once she finished her training, he would be reassigned.

"Nope," Hazelton said. "I have a car outside that will drop you off at the airport. We even have a plane waiting for you, courtesy of Sheikh Ali. And by the way, do not try to come back. You are now officially on the Do-Not-Fly-List. This is America, jerk face, land of the free. You can stuff your misogynistic attitude and your Sharia Law where the sun don't shine."

Hope stepped back and smiled. "Thanks, Hazelton. I could just shoot him in the balls and be done with it, but I guess deportation is a better option."

Hazelton smirked. "No problem, *pipsqueak*. Life's been pretty boring without you around. Good thing we've been tracking this guy." He jerked the man toward him. "You'd better go back to your date. He's looking rather pale." Hazelton pulled the now squirming man toward the exit.

Just as they reached the doorway, Rami turned and glared at Hope. "This isn't over, *princess*! You were promised to me, and I *will* enforce that contract."

Hazelton growled, "Damn, I should have let her shoot you in the balls." Then he yanked at him even harder and tossed him through the doorway.

Hope turned back to her table and Tom, who was standing with his hand poised over the gun he wore in a holster under his leather jacket. Her face reddened and she sighed, "Sorry about that. Just a little misunderstanding." She grabbed his hand and tugged. "Come on, the bill's already been paid. Let's scoot."

Tom nodded. He frowned. "Why did he call you Amal?"

"Amal is Arabic for Hope, or rather Hope is the English translation of Amal. I haven't been called Amal for a very long time. Not since I came to America." She turned and let him out the door.

"And who was that guy?"

Hope muttered, "No one." She continued to pull him toward the door.

"And what about the other guy? The one who grabbed him. He looked like the Secret Service."

"Not *now*, Tom."

She pushed him through the door.

Once they were settled into Hope's car, Tom turned and studied her. "So, who was the big guy? The dude who looked like he was a federal agent."

"Warren Hazelton, former U.S. Navy Seal, special ops. He's been my bodyguard since I moved here. By agreement with my father and Cade, he still protects me—from a discreet distance—when I leave Agency property." She scrunched up her nose. "Sorry I didn't tell you. I didn't want to make you feel self-conscious. I wanted this to just be about us."

Tom nodded. "I can see how he could put a crimp in things." He smiled. "But if you can pretend he isn't observing our every move, so can I. Though I may eventually have to buy him a blindfold."

Hope laughed, then grabbed him by the ears and kissed him.

He pulled away.

Hope frowned.

"And what's this about a fiancé?"

Hope sighed and sat back. "He's not my fiancé, at least not anymore. My grandfather was the head of our tribe or family in Saudi Arabia. He believed in Sharia Law and arranged marriages. Technically, as head of our tribe and as my grandfather, he had the authority to arrange a marriage for me. The problem was, he and my father were estranged. In fact, my grandfather had put a price on my dad's head, which is part of the reason we sought asylum in the United States. Plus, we're Christian, not Muslim. We give no credence to Sharia Law."

"So, what's the deal with the marriage contract?"

"After we moved here, my grandfather threatened to take me back to Saudi Arabia and raise me in accordance with Sharia Law. I'm not going to go into what that would have meant for me, but I will say I would have rather died than submit to it or him. Despite outward appearances, women are still chattel in the Middle East. All the shiny office buildings and luxurious shopping malls won't change that. I would have been stripped of my rights and my freedom and forced to live under my husband's thumb. Every man's thumb, really. My grandfather was murdered before he could carry out the threat, but apparently, not before he and Rami's family entered into a marriage contract."

"My God, is that even legal? How could he do that without your consent?"

"In this country, it *isn't* legal. In Saudi Arabia, it's a bit murkier. However, no one has produced a written contract, so they have no actual proof. And once my grandfather died, my father became head of the tribe. His first act was to nullify all outstanding marriage contracts. In fact, he made marriage contracts illegal. His second was to renounce his inheritance and his title, and pass it on to my uncle, his brother, Azar, with the understanding that the marriage contract ban would stand."

"So, Rami has no standing, here or in Saudi Arabia?"

"As far as I know, but that won't stop him from pursuing the claim."

"Why would he do that?"

Hope laughed. "Why do most want to marry royalty? It's rarely for love. More often it's for influence, prestige, power, and money — lots and lots of money." She gazed at Tom. "Seriously, for the most part, being a royal sucks. No one in their right mind would want to switch places with me."

Tom flushed. "I hope you know I don't need or want your money. I'm not a trust fund baby or anything, but I have access to plenty of —"

Hope held up her hand to silence him. She asked softly, "What *do* you want, Tom?"

"You." He leaned over and kissed her. "And these lips. God, I love your luscious lips. So sweet, for such a dirty mouth."

Tom grabbed his bottle of beer and drank deeply. "And then this guy, Rami says, *This isn't over, princess! You were promised to me and I will enforce that contract.* I almost took his head off."

Anders laughed. "Shit. I know it's not funny, but damn.

That's only a small part of what Hope has been through. When she was fourteen, someone tried to kidnap her off the streets of Dubai. They took down her bodyguards and then went after her. Hope grabbed a chair from a nearby café and fended them off like a lion tamer. She knew they wouldn't shoot her. They wanted her to get to her father. She was of no value if she was dead. Hope raised enough of a ruckus that others came to her aid until the police arrived."

Tom scowled. "It's bad enough that she's a princess. Crap, how I am supposed to deal with that? I'm just a cowboy raised on a ranch in Montana."

Anders snorted. "Yeah, one of the most profitable beef producers in North America. You're hardly poor. Besides, Hope doesn't care about money. If she did, she wouldn't have joined the Agency. And believe me, she fought tooth and nail to get in."

"Still, she attracts trouble. Shit, going out into the field with her is going to be risky. Not only will we have to deal with the danger stemming from our assignments, but she has all this baggage that's is likely to pop up when we least expect it. What if Rami or someone else from her crazy family shows up in the middle of a takedown or an undercover operation? We'll be toast."

"Part of Hope's baggage is her cover."

"What?"

"Think about it. She's a fucking princess who looks like she's maybe one hundred pounds soaking wet. Who's going to seriously believe she's an undercover agent? In fact, Cade is considering giving me my own team, and if I get it, Hope's going to be part of it. As are you and Cate. The plan is to hide in plain sight, warts and all. We'll have to get day jobs, but they will be jobs that put us in the places where we need ears."

"How is that even remotely a good idea? What about our families? That will make them targets."

"As we see it, they already are. Think about it. Cate's family is incredibly wealthy and her mom is a big muckety muck in the U.S. government. Hope's parents are famous lawyers and her dad is a sheikh. Your dad is an icon in corporate America. All the agents in my team will have family connections that make them visible, yet invisible to our targets. The children of the wealthy are often discounted as hapless fools who couldn't survive in the real world without a trust fund."

Tom cocked an eyebrow. "What's your connection?"

"My dad's an Admiral. In the U.S. Navy."

Tom stared at him for a moment, then picked up his beer and drained the bottle. "Hokay, then. To the outside world, we're a bunch of entitled trust fund babies."

"And to our targets, we're the devil in disguise."

CHAPTER FOUR: TESTED

Hope jogged once around the obstacle course, then dove into the *Arctic Channel*. She kept her arms pinned to her sides and slid through the webbed plastic with ease, using only her legs to propel her forward. When she reached the other side, she pushed off from the bottom and popped up through the ice to the surface. Hope grabbed the side, pulled herself out, shed the harness around her shoulders, and began to run.

Dianna moved with her as she sprinted to the *Tunnel of Tears*. Hope launched herself onto the floor, her wet body sliding halfway in. Pulling on the handrails on the bottom and sides of the tunnel, she shot out the other end.

Then she ran hard, pumping her arms, barely bending to scoop up the high jump pole. She planted the pole on the ground and launched herself into the air. Hope just missed clearing the wall. She grabbed at the rope with both hands, latched on, and crawled over to the other side.

Hope heard Dianna shouting but ignored her. She didn't care if Dianna was chastising her or cheering. She had a job to do and she intended to get it done. She cautiously slid down the climbing wall, hanging onto the rope until she could safely jump to the ground. Avoiding the mud pool in front of her, she ran around it and raced to the row of inner tubes.

Dianna was shouting even more loudly now. Hope continued to ignore her. Distraction was her enemy. She stopped and carefully wiped her hands and feet on the dry grass. Then she leaped onto the plateau of inner tubes.

Her legs spread wide, Hope danced lightly along the left side of the structure, leaping over those that flipped or collapsed beneath her. On several occasions, she used her left leg to push back up from the ground onto the tires. She again stopped and ensured that her hands and feet were dry.

Hope ran to *Monkey Death* and grabbed the first bar, swinging quickly through the bars and twisted shapes. At the end, she slithered down a metal pole and landed hard on the top of the catapult. She was thrown into the air, and just before landing, did a flip and landed on her feet directly in front of five large men dressed as Ninjas. At this point, she heard Dianna hooting and clapping. That gave Hope the boost her tired body needed.

Ignoring the large men, Hope ran between them, ducking away from arms that reached and legs that kicked out. She slapped the bell and collapsed to the ground, breathing heavily. Hope took a couple of deep breaths, then sat up. "I did it, I did it!" she exclaimed. "I fucking did it!"

Dianna ran to her, a wide smile on her face. "And where the hell did you learn to do *that*?"

Hope giggled. "Anders told me how to handle each obstacle, and after that, I went into the training center to watch his tapes. I figured out how to use my size to my advantage. I didn't know if it would work, but I had to try." She rolled around the grass, laughing with delight. Hope flopped on her back and spread her arms wide. Softly she said, "Anders told me there were no rules, that I just had to successfully work my way through the obstacles. So that's what I did."

Dianna's eyes narrowed. "And you never snuck out here to practice?"

Hope sat up and smiled at Dianna. "Nope. A lot of this stuff is just playground equipment for adults. I let my inner child take over and allowed my body to respond with rote memory. If you shut your head down and stop thinking about the consequences, it's easy."

"You got through the *Arctic Channel* in record time. One point three minutes."

Hope blushed. "They had a similar underwater water maze at a hotel in Dubai. The less you moved, the faster you slid through it. I just went into mermaid mode, you know, swimming only by moving my legs." She waved her hand. "For once, my age was an advantage. Unlike you old farts, I still remember what it was like to play as a child."

Dianna's mouth quirked up in a half smile, which quickly vanished. "And the *Tunnel of Tears*?"

"Water slides. Run, jump, and slide."

"What about the inner tubes? You showed amazing balance and dexterity. You looked like you were dancing."

"I was. My ballet teacher had this exercise where we leaped around the floor, bouncing off hard and soft objects she had hidden under a sheet. She wanted us to rely on our instincts to maintain our balance. So that one was *Ballet One Zero One*."

Dianna cocked her head. "How did you manage that little trick with the catapult?"

"High School P.E. Learned how to twist in the air when dismounting from the parallel bars." Her mouth curved up and she said sarcastically, "Probably the only useful thing I learned in that class. Anyway, I figured the catapult was lined up right. All I needed to do was land on my feet and run straight ahead."

Dianna frowned. "What about the final obstacle? The Ninjas?"

"Hey, you never said I had to fight them. You said I had to get through them and hit the bell. They were expecting me to engage, so I didn't." Hope peered up at her. "So, did I pass?"

Dianna laughed. "I guess so." She glanced at her stopwatch. "And in record time. Dammit, people are going to be watching that tape for months, if not years." She gazed at

Hope. "If you are able to rely on your instincts in the field like you just did on this course, you'll do fine. It's when you're overthinking it or afraid that you might have a problem."

Hope nodded. "I know. I'm working on that."

Dianna studied her, then sighed. "I just hope overconfidence doesn't bite you in the ass, Hope. Remember, you're human. You *can* break." Dianna pulled her long blonde ponytail off her neck and blew out a breath. "I guess it's time for your field test, then. I'll schedule it. Remember, it won't be announced. You probably won't even know you're in it until after it's started." She smirked. "Good luck. You're going to need it. They don't play fair."

Hope and Tom left the bar located right outside the Agency compound. She gazed at him and smiled. "Too bad we have to go back to the dorms. It would be nice to spend some time really alone." She shot Tom a shy smile. "Everyone was watching us in there. That was uncomfortable."

Tom grinned. "Well, Ms. Perfect. You beat the advanced obstacle course in one try. Something no one else has done. Now everyone's trying to figure out what makes you so special. You've got the men checking their *equipment*, trying to figure out if they've been robbed of their balls, while the women are all cheering."

Hope frowned. "I didn't do it to best anyone. I did it to prove to myself that I could. There's a big difference. What was I supposed to do? Fail, so the men felt better?"

Tom snorted. "Only thing worse than being bested by a woman is being the object of her pity." He stopped walking and hugged Hope. "I, for one, am completely and unconditionally proud of you." He brushed his lips with hers. "Now you just need to pass the field exercise. And I'm sure it's going to be a humdinger. You need to be alert at all times, because they like to take Probies by surprise. They are especially fond of attacking while a Probie is taking a shower or is sound asleep."

Hope stared at him. "That's awful."

Tom nodded. "Just don't sleep naked. That could be embarrassing. However, it's a good test of how you'll respond when suddenly and unexpectedly faced with danger."

Hope smiled. "How did they take you?"

"On the basketball court. With three other guys. Five armed men surrounded us, slipped burlap bags over our heads, and removed us from the scene. They literally dragged us from the court and threw us into the back of a truck. I almost wet my pants. Then they separated us and put us in interrogation rooms. They questioned me with the hood still on. I was hot and extremely uncomfortable."

Hope smiled at him. "Did they waterboard you or something?"

"No, thank God. Though that room was stifling, so a little water in the face would have been welcome."

"So, what happened? How did you escape?"

"Those guys never went off-script. They pretended to be terrorists. Claimed they were looking for Infidels to exchange for some guy lodged at Guantanamo Bay. It took a while before I realized it wasn't real. Once I figured that out, I settled down because I wasn't in any real danger. I just had to get out of there in one piece without getting caught." He paused and smiled. "They tossed me into a cell, and I saved a plastic knife from the first meal they served me — which was some crappy beef on toast by the way. I used it to pick the lock. Damn thing kept breaking on me, but that final shard sprang the lock. Then they came at me full on. I figured they had cameras on us waiting for someone to make a move. They tried to gang up on me, but by then, I was pissed. Somehow, I managed to take all of them down. Man, they did not go easy on me. I had bruises for weeks. But I finally escaped."

"Once you got out of the building, did they pursue you?"

Tom shook his head. "Not that I was aware of, but I was running away pretty hard. Then I realized where I was and knew I was home free."

"Where were you?"

Tom chuckled. "In that wooded area at the end of the compound. The one with the jogging trail. There's this shed tucked into the corner. They must have dressed it up inside to look like a prison. Once I got my bearings, I ran to Cade's office and reported in. Was he surprised!"

He smiled at Hope. "I imagine they have something much more challenging in mind for you." He playfully swiped at her chin.

"But you aced it?"

"Not exactly."

Hope stared at him. "What? Why not?"

"I got a big old lecture about leaving the others behind. I was ordered to go back and free them. That was the hard part. Once I escaped, they had doubled the number of the guards and moved the guys to a different area. I had a hell of a time finding them, and when I did, I had a battle on my hands. I had to take all of the guards down before I could get anyone else out. Then some of the guys refused to leave. Said they'd rather sit in the cell than get shot while trying to escape."

"Wow. They thought it was real?"

"Yup. That made no sense. We all knew what was coming."

"So, what did you do?"

"I left them there. I had given them the option and they refused. I figured that was all I could be expected to do. They were putting the others in jeopardy, which was counterproductive, so I figured it was better to cut our losses and get out." He grinned "Besides, I knew no harm would come to them. It wasn't real." Tom smirked. "Funny thing. The guys who stayed behind disappeared. Not sure if they were kicked out or left on their own to crawl out. The situation was pretty scary, at first, but I thought it was pretty obvious that it was all a game." He shrugged. "Guess that's why they do the field test. To separate the wheat from the chaff. Not everyone reacts well to that kind of stress."

Hope groaned. "I can only imagine what they have in store for me."

Tom kissed her. "Nothing you can't handle, I'm sure." Suddenly, there was a loud *thwack* and Tom dropped to the ground.

Hope stared down at him, then at the man who had struck him in the head with a pistol. She assumed a defensive stance and waited for the man to come at her. He smirked and stepped back. Distracted by his movements, Hope didn't realize another person had slipped behind her until someone grabbed her by the hair and thrust a rag over her mouth and nose. As Hope slowly slipped into unconsciousness, she thought, "Damn, the Agency got me!"

Hope awoke in a dark room. She tried to sit up, then realized her arms and legs were bound to the legs of a cot. *Oh, this is so not funny, guys!* She tugged at her restraints to determine whether they had any give. *Obviously, these bozos have no experience with rope. I can slip out of these easily.* She began to work her way out of her restraints, then realized that she had also been gagged. *Really?*

A man entered the room. Hope stilled and peered at him. He was well-cloaked in the shadows, making it difficult for her to see him. She waited. The man moved. And with growing dread, she realized he was dressed in a thawb, the traditional white gown Arab men wore. Inwardly, she groaned. *Maybe this isn't an Agency exercise. Maybe this is real.*

"Hello, Amal," the man said in Arabic. "Welcome to my dungeon, where you will stay until you see reason."

Terror fought its way into her mind. *Rami?* She pulled on her restraints, rocking the cot as she tried to speak around her gag.

Rami laughed. It was a cruel laugh. "I see, now you wish to speak, Amal? Too little, too late. I permitted you to function freely among the Infidels, but you cast me aside. So now, we will do it my way."

He turned, and she heard the distinctive click of a door closing. Rami had left the room.

Hope stilled. *Okay, girl. This is real. Heck, you might even be in Saudi Arabia already. Think!* She inventoried her clothing. The sundress she had been wearing was gone. In its place was a black abaya, the gown worn by Arab women. Slowly, she smiled. *My clothing may be gone, but I'm guessing they didn't touch my underwear. And that's where I store my ultimate weapon.* Hope peered into the darkness. She could see no cameras. No other watchers. Cautiously, she pulled at the ropes that bound each wrist until she could slip her hands free. Then Hope sat up and tugged on the rope that bound her feet. She quickly untied the knots and tossed the rope onto the floor. She stilled and listened. Silence. Hope yanked at her gag and listened again. It was deathly quiet. She was alone.

Hope massaged her wrists, then stood and walked to the door. It was a simple knob lock. Old Rami must have expected no resistance. *The fool.* Sure, he didn't know about her Agency training, but a knob lock was child's play, even to a civilian. She pushed on it to make sure it was actually locked, then reached under the abaya and tugged at the bottom of her bra, removing the underwire from the slit she had cut in the lining. In one swift movement, she punched out the lock from the other side of the door. *This is way too easy.*

Carefully, Hope slipped the door open an inch and gazed outside. *What the?* She could hear traffic, cars honking. And there were no guards. She moved outside the room and looked around. Her intended prison was nothing more than a basement storage locker. She heard footsteps and quickly pulled back into the room. The footsteps stopped at the door. Someone jiggled the handle and she heard a giggle.

"Hope? Are you in there? Don't shoot. It's Cate."

Shit. The dummy didn't even take her out of the country? Hope pulled the door open and smiled at her friend. "That was fast."

"Tracked you through the Agency medical chip." Her eyes narrowed. "Did they even bother to tie you up?"

"Bunch of amateurs. Used single knots. Slipped out of those, grabbed my trusty underwire, and punched the lock. I was just about to make a run for it." Her eyes narrowed. "It was Rami. I thought they deported him."

Cate frowned. "Probably slipped back in through the Mexican border. It's not like it's well-protected. That border has more holes than Swiss cheese. If he'd tried to come in via Canada, the Mounties would have caught him. With his dark skin and dark hair, he really would have stood out. Down south, he probably blended right in."

Cate pushed her back into the room and shut the door. She hugged her. "I am so proud of you. You did half my job for me." Cate pulled away and dropped her backpack on the floor. She gestured toward Hope's gown. "There is no way you can run in that. I brought you some clothes and a Kevlar vest, as well as a gun. We don't know how many *unfriendlies* are involved."

Hope laughed. "Trust me, not many. Rami can't risk getting anyone other than his friends involved. They're all a bunch of knotheads. His father is going to be furious when he finds out." She pulled the abaya over her head and tossed it onto the floor. Then she slipped on jeans, a sweatshirt, and a gun holster. "Did you come in alone?"

Cate shook her head. She handed Hope a pistol. "Tom's watching the entrance. This is storage for residents of an apartment building owned by a consortium of Saudi investors. There's only one way in or out of the storage lockers. We need to run through an open hallway, but Anders has a car right outside. We were supposed to confirm your location, then assess. I never expected your door to be unlocked." Cate rolled her eyes. "You probably didn't even need us."

Hope smirked. "Hey, I do need a getaway car." She pushed her ear against the door, then opened it a crack. She held the pistol up and slid outside. "Showtime. Let's blow this pop stand." Hope pushed in the knob lock and slammed the door. Then she and Cate ran.

They burst through the outer door onto the street, where Tom stood with his gun drawn, his expression menacing. Hope giggled and he stepped down, smiling. He grabbed her hand and led them to a car idling by the curb. Tom pushed Hope into the back seat and moved in next to her. Cate jumped into the front. "Let's roll," she yelled.

Anders grunted and pulled away.

Hope took a deep breath and smiled at Tom. "Guess this wasn't my field test, huh?"

Tom shook his head, revealing a bandage on the back.

"Oh, crap, they hurt you?"

"Not really, he was only out for a minute or two before coming to," Anders said. "He hurt his head when he hit the sidewalk. Guy needs to learn how to fall gracefully."

"Hey!" Tom said.

Cate laughed. "His pride is hurt. Anyway, he was lucky there were so many people around. There were witnesses. We knew almost immediately that you had been taken."

Hope took Tom's hand and kissed it. "I think we were a little distracted. We weren't really paying attention. Give him a break. So, where are we?"

"Near Embassy Row," Tom said. "D.C. Some apartment complex for embassy employees." Tom pulled her into a hug.

"But you wouldn't have been there long. Rami contacted someone and asked to borrow a jet. Don't know if he succeeded, but one way or the other, your intended destination was Saudi Arabia. Your father and Cade already have the private charters terminal staked out. If they'd missed you, they intended to go after Rami themselves."

"Give me your phone."

Tom handed it to her and she punched in Cade's number.

"This had better be good news," Cade growled when he answered.

"Um, can I speak to my father, please?"

"Hope? You're safe?"

"Free as a bird. Let me talk to my dad."

Cade spoke to someone, and then she heard her father's voice. "Hope? Are you okay? Did that little shit force himself on you?"

"You know better than that, Dad. But we need to get Rami out of the picture. Permanently. I can't have him interfering with my life. This was a sloppy attempt and it failed, but if he had managed to get me to Saudi Arabia, there could have been real trouble. It's time to shut him down."

Sheikh Harun Ali muffled the phone and said something to Cade. Then he came back on the line. "Kid doesn't have diplomatic immunity, so Cade will have him arrested for attempted kidnapping. He will be tried, convicted, and deported, with notice to his father, his government, and the media. A very public shaming is what he deserves. And a little time in jail might do him some good. Meanwhile, it may not be safe for you on the streets alone. God knows what his friends would do. They're all a bunch of idiots. Why didn't you call Hazelton for backup before going off the compound? You need to be more careful."

"Dad, we were less than a block from home base. There were military types everywhere. I can't believe Rami managed to pull this off. He must have had help. Competent help."

Her father grunted. "Well, there isn't much that money can't buy. I have my suspicions. I need to check a few things out." He paused. "You're going to have to put up with Hazelton until we figure this out. And call your mother. She was ready to go after Rami herself. And you know *she* would have shot him in the balls."

"And deprive me of that privilege?" Hope laughed. "I don't think so. Later, Dad. Love you."

Her father emitted a sigh. "Love you, too. Stay safe, kiddo." He disconnected.

Tom cupped her chin and smiled. Then he kissed her. "That was the longest twelve hours of my life."

Hope laughed. "I can think of better ways to end a date, that's for sure."

He kissed her again. "Speaking of that . . ."

Hope awoke to darkness. In murky grey of dawn, she could just barely make out the time on her phone. Five AM. With a deep sigh, she rolled out of bed and stretched. Still sleepy, she pulled on her running shorts, tee-shirt, and a jacket. She stuffed a fanny pack with her phone, whistle, gun, and pepper spray, and fastened it around her waist. Then she stepped into her socks and shoes and made her way to the front door of the dormitory. At the last minute, she veered from her chosen path and walked into the cafeteria.

Buzzy, the chef, looked up from the shelves he was filling with just-baked cinnamon rolls and smiled. "You're up early, girl," he drawled. "Heard old Tom took you out to dinner and got you snatched." He shook his head and laughed. "Those young dudes just don't know how to treat women right. In my day, a woman was pampered and protected." His eyes narrowed as Hope grabbed a plate with a roll and a bottle of water. "Since when do you eat before you run?"

Hope sank into a chair by a nearby table and nibbled on the warm bun. She smirked. "Thought I'd break up my routine. I'm pretty sure today's going to be my field test. I need to go in well-fed and with some supplies. Can I get some eggs over easy, dry wheat toast, and bacon, please? Then I'll need some protein bars, an apple, and a bottle of water for the road. Not sure what's going to happen, but I intend to be ready."

Buzzy nodded and turned away, humming the Marine Corp Hymn.

Hope sat up straighter and listened. Was Buzzy giving her a clue? There was a Marine base about fifty clicks from the training center, and it was surrounded by some rugged terrain. She pulled out her phone and began scanning area maps, noting entry and exit points. Damn, that would be a great place to dump her, test her survival skills. Usually they dumped people in a warehouse somewhere, bound and gagged, but she had already been there, done that. They would provide a different scenario, something more extreme.

Buzzy placed a plate before her and set down several protein bars, another bottle of water, and an apple. "Good luck," he whispered with a wink.

Hope dug into her breakfast while studying more maps on her phone. What would she need in the woods? Matches? Flares? An Army knife? She knew she could be grabbed anytime. She wouldn't have time to go back to her room. Hope finished her breakfast and hurried into the kitchen. "Buzzy, I need some supplies."

Buzzy nodded toward a closet. "Go ahead, but anything you find in there probably won't help."

Hope hurried to the supply closet and stuffed a pack of matches and a votive candle into her fanny pack. She grabbed two utility knives in sheaths and stuffed one into each sock. *I may not be able to hang onto any of this stuff, but maybe if I hide it on my body, they won't find it.*

When Hope exited the supply closet, Dianna was standing next to Buzzy. She smiled at Hope and checked her watch. "Ten, nine, eight, seven, six . . ."

Hope began to feel woozy. She glared at Buzzy. "Dammit, you—" Hope slumped to the floor.

CHAPTER FIVE: THE GREAT ESCAPE

"And she's out." Dianna smirked. "Great job, Buzzy. Putting a sleeping pill in her cinnamon roll was a nice touch."

"Anders figured they'd never be able to grab her on the street. She's already on her guard. We were going to do it at lunch, but when she ducked into the cafeteria, it all just fell into place." He motioned toward Hope. "She was stocking up before you got here. You gonna empty her pockets and that fanny pack?"

Dianna nodded her head. "Rules say we remove all weapons and her phone but leave everything else. We're going to stash her in an old cabin in the hills near Bears Den Park. She's going to have to break out and find her way home. Did you throw her off with the Marine Corp Hymn?"

"Yup. She fell for it. Saw her checking maps. She thinks she's headed to Quantico."

"Good. She'll be about two hours away. That should be enough to confuse her. Did you place your bet with Harper?"

Buzzy grinned. "Yup. I bet she outlasts you. Passes the twenty-four-hour mark without being caught. My Hope is no dummy. Once she wakes up, she'll escape in no time. And then she'll find someone to help her. That kid knows how to wrap people around her little finger."

Dianna grinned. "We'll see. We've got all sorts of surprises in store for her."

Buzzy frowned. "What if she gets hurt?"

"She'll be under surveillance twenty-four-seven. We don't

want her dead, just challenged."

Tom and Anders walked into the kitchen.

Tom stared at Hope's motionless body on the floor. "What the hell did you give her? She's conked."

"Just a little sleeping pill. We want her a little dopey when she wakes up. We need to know whether she can push through." Dianna smiled and handed Anders a set of keys. "She shouldn't wake for at least four hours. The cabin is ready. Surveillance in the cabin and the surrounding area is set up. Put her on a chair, tie her hands behind her and her feet to the legs. And bolt the door to cabin from the outside. She has to figure out how to get past it. And make sure you strip that cabin down before she wakes."

Anders nodded. "Who's handling the drone?"

"Carmichael," Dianna replied. "He'll be set up in a tree stand nearby."

"How far to the nearest road?" Tom asked.

"About seven miles. She can run that easily, but first she has to figure out which direction to head, and that will be hard without traffic noise. She'll also have to dodge all the Agency operatives on her way out. She may ultimately get her bearings, but she won't have a clear path to the road." She grinned. "And once she hits the road, we have even more surprises in store."

Tom shook his head. "Does she even have a flashlight? She's going to be wandering around in those woods in the dark. That's not exactly safe. There are bears and other wildlife. What if she falls and gets hurt?"

Dianna rolled her eyes. "She has ten more hours of daylight. "She'll be fine. Besides, the drone will be following her the whole time. We'll know where she is and if she needs help. Give the girl a chance."

Hope groaned. Slowly, she opened her eyes. Everything was one big blur. She closed her eyes and tried to clear her head. She breathed in, then out. *Relax. Assess. Act.* Hope stilled and listened. Birds chirping. The wind gently batting the walls. She breathed in again. It smelled like she was in the woods. She opened her eyes, fluttering them until her vision cleared. Her gaze swept the room. A cabin. A bunk bed with no linens. A kitchen with a water pump and wood stove. No refrigerator.

Hope tried to move. She was seated on a heavy wooden chair. Hands tied behind her. Her legs tied to the chair. She tried to kick out, but her legs didn't move. *Okay then. Let's try the hands.* Hope pulled at the rope that bound her wrists. She twisted and yanked until she felt some give. She pulled her wrists away from each other, creating more give. *All I need is a half-inch. Come on.* Patiently, she twisted and yanked. Then she manipulated one hand, flattening her fingers, then bunching them together to give her more room. Gently, she pulled one hand free, then the other.

Hope brought her arms around to the front and pulled off the rest of the rope. She shook out her wrists to regain circulation, then wrapped the rope around her waist and knotted it. *One never knows when a rope will be required, does one?*

She reached for the rope binding her legs to the chair. *Hmmm. Knotted tight. In several places. Not quite as easy.* She untied her shoes and tried to pull her feet free, but the harder she pulled, the tighter the rope felt. She again gazed around the room. Her fanny pack had been placed on the bed. *If I could just reach that . . .* Hope began to rock the chair, trying to force it on its side.

When she fell to the floor, she heard a *clunk.* The sound only a hard object made. *What was that?* Hope reached for her sock and felt around the ankle then began to giggle. A utility knife had fallen into her shoe. Her captors had missed it.

Hope pulled the sock free of the rope and reached inside. She wedged out the knife and pulled it from its sheath. She sawed through the rope, and it fell to the ground.

Hope scrambled to her knees and slowly stood. She swayed slightly, then regained her balance. She blinked hard. *Damn, I feel like I have a hangover. What did they give me?* She shook it off. She righted the chair and grabbed her shoes, then sat and pulled them on, quickly tying the laces.

Fimally, Hope stood. *Okay, next step, surveillance. Kill the cameras.* She peered around the room, then returned to her chair. *They would want a clear line of sight.* She slowly turned her body in the chair, looking for a small box or object. *There. On the window sill. And on the lamp by the bed.*

Hope walked to each, removed them and threw them in the chemical toilet in the corner. She gazed down at her clothing. *Dammit, why did I wear bright yellow? I need to blend in, not stand out.* She pulled off her jacket and turned it inside out. At least the reverse side was beige. She pulled it back over her head, then scowled at her running shorts. There wasn't much she could do about them. Maybe the beige would be enough to confuse her watchers.

Hope moved to the only door and pushed on it. There was no give. *I'll bet they bolted it shut from the outside.*

She walked to two small windows on the opposite wall. Hope could see that nails had been hammered in around the frame. She slowly walked around the cabin, opening a closet and a few drawers in the kitchen area. All were empty. She picked up the pole lamp. It was pretty flimsy, but it just might be heavy enough to break a window.

She pulled the lamp cord from the outlet and set it down next to the window. Hope walked to the toilet and relieved herself. Then she went to the sink, pumped water until it ran clear, and drank deeply, using her hands as a cup. After drying her fingers on her running shorts, she grabbed her fanny pack and examined the contents. They had removed her gun, pepper spray, whistle, and phone, but her protein bars, water bottle, matches, and candle remained. Hope fastened the pack around her waist and placed the utility knife inside. She sidled up to the window and peered out. The area outside was covered with bramble and bushes. There was no one in sight.

Hope picked up the lamp and began to ram the bottom against the glass. It broke easily. She continued to bang on it until all of the glass was broken out of the frame. She grabbed the flimsy mattress from one of the bunks and on the underside discovered a listening device. *Dammit.* She smashed it and pulled the mattress over to the window. Hope stood on the chair and pushed the mattress through the shattered frame onto the top of the bushes. She grabbed the second mattress and rolled it up so it fit into the window frame. *That should be sufficient to protect me from most of the broken glass and bramble.*

Just as she was about to crawl out the window, she saw a glint in the distance. Sun bouncing off metal. Hope peered at it. The wind shifted and through the trees, she saw someone in a tree stand. Then she heard a soft whir. She stuck her head out of the window and spotted a small drone, hovering overhead.

Hope pulled back into the cabin and smiled. She could use the drone to find her way out of here, but first, she had to disable the operator. Hope crawled through the window, dropped on top of the mattress and rolled to the ground. She stood and ignored the drone. *First confuse, then diffuse.* Hope darted for the cover of some low-lying trees and began to crawl toward the tree stand. *Ouch! I wish I had worn long pants. I'm going to scratch the shit out of my legs.* She could hear the drone hovering, moving back and forth, bumping into branches, trying to find her.

When she got to the tree holding the drone operator, she peered up through the brush. The man was frantically manipulating the controls, glancing at a small screen, his face scrunched in confusion. Hope moved behind him. Using the steps nailed into the trunk, she scrambled up the tree. The man began to turn just as she jumped into the stand. She poked him in the back with the handle of her utility knife and growled, "Don't move, or I'll cut you into teeny tiny pieces. I'm sure there are some hungry bears around here somewhere."

The man set down the remote control and slowly raised his hands. "Dammit, Ali, I'm supposed to be the predator. You're the prey."

Hope laughed. "Change in plans, bucko." She stuffed the knife into her jacket pocket and pulled the rope from around her waist. "Now, set that drone down carefully. If you break it, I imagine the Agency will take its replacement out of your paycheck."

The man carefully complied and raised his hands again. Hope looped the rope around his wrists and pulled tight, then tied his still upstretched arms to a large tree branch.

The man began to yell, "Mayday! Prey has compromised . . ."

"Oh, enough of that!" Hope exclaimed. She bunted him on the side of the head, and he slumped in his chair. She grabbed the controller and the screen and perched beside the motionless man. Hope played with the controls until the drone hovered directly in front of her. Then she sent it straight up into the sky. Watching the screen, she manipulated the drone, pointing it north, south, east, and west. Okay, two roads. One creek. Numerous trails. She pointed the drone toward the east. That appeared to be a hiking trail. She pointed the drone to the west. Another hiking trail, but not as distinct. They probably expected her to take the clear path. She grinned. *West it is.*

Hope landed the drone in the tree stand and turned off the controller. She removed the batteries from each and tossed them into the trees. After setting the equipment at the agent's feet, she hustled back down the trunk of the tree, then ran west.

Several hours later, Hope backed up against a tree and bent to touch her toes. She was becoming tired. It was time for a break. She pulled the bottle of water from her fanny pack and drank deeply. She had charted an uneven path, hoping to avoid any surprises along the way. Walking parallel to the hiking trail and occasionally crossing to the other side, she had carefully picked through rocks, fallen branches, and other forest debris, avoiding the occasional hiker—who might or might not have been Agency personnel attempting to track her. While she knew they could monitor her with the medical chip implanted near her wrist, that was supposedly barred except for emergencies, like if she didn't return after twenty-four hours. Bad guys wouldn't have access to that chip, and in this instance, the Agency was the bad guy.

Hope pulled a protein bar from her pack and munched, carefully scanning her surroundings. The path had been relatively quiet. It was a weekday, so families and other more dedicated hikers had been scarce. That had made it easy to hear and avoid other people on the trail. Sound traveled in a dense forest. The only mistake she had made thus far was failing to take the communications device out of drone-boy's ear. She had been in too much of a hurry. That little device would have helped immensely in learning the whereabouts of her trackers.

Still, she could hear people moving through the forest far in advance. Twice she had scrambled up a tree to avoid someone. From that position, she had seen the road she was seeking. Two men in camouflage were hunkered down near there, obviously waiting for her. She would need to go around them, then find someone with a phone so she could call for a ride.

Hope placed the protein bar wrapper and water bottle back

in her pack and stood. No way was she leaving a trail. She stirred the ground where she had been sitting to eliminate evidence of her rest stop. Then she studied the sun and headed northwest, away from the hiking trail. It would be dark soon, and much harder to discreetly flag down someone on the road. She needed to reach it quickly.

As she moved away, Hope heard the crunch of leaves, then someone softly swearing as they tripped over a branch. *Cate.* Cate would have a com in her ear, and if Hope could snatch it, she'd know where everyone else was. And Cate would also have a phone and a weapon. As much as Hope hated to jump her roommate and friend, this was all a game. Her only goal was to get back to the Agency playground in one piece, outside the twenty-four-hour requirement.

Hope slipped behind a large tree trunk and waited. Cate slowly walked past her, trying to be stealthy. Hope withdrew her utility knife and snuck up behind her, purposely stepping on a branch, the loud snap forcing Cate to whip around, her weapon raised. Hope ducked and went for Cate's legs, knocking them out from under her, then she pushed two fingers to her neck, immobilizing her. Hope removed Cate's holster, weapon, and tool belt and fastened them to her body. Then she removed zip ties from the tool belt and bound Cate's ankles and wrists.

"Sorry, Sista," Hope said softly. "One of us had to go down. Better you than me." She pulled the communications device from Cate's ear, wiped it down with a wet nap, and placed it in her own ear. She could clearly hear Tom and Anders, which meant they were close. Quickly, Hope slipped back into the forest and listened to their conversation as they searched for her.

Within minutes, she reached the road. She stopped and listened as one by one, the searchers checked in. She was surrounded. Her only option would be to get away from the forest and the road before calling for help. She peered down the road, first left, then right. To her left, about five hundred feet away, a forestry services truck sat on the side of the road. It appeared to be empty. To her right, further up the road, she saw movement. That was where they were waiting for her. Unless the truck was a trap.

Covering her mouth with her hand to muffle her voice, Hope whispered into the com, "Guys. I've got her! She's up a tree. About one klick from me. She's still wearing her yellow running clothes. And she's watching. Be careful."

"I'm behind her," Anders said.

"So am I," Tom added. "Let's sandbag her. Cate, you distract her. Make some noise so she won't hear us approaching. Mark and Harry, block the path ahead in case she tries to run. She's a sneaky little shit. I wouldn't put it past her to swing from tree to tree like a damn monkey."

Hope attempted to stifle a laugh. *Oh, you are so going to pay for that, darling.* She sensed movement to her right. Good. The sentries were moving away. She waited a few minutes. Then she tossed the com into the brush—no sense in giving her position away—and nonchalantly walked to the other side of the road.

She crept up to the back of the truck. It was empty. She moved to the side and peered into the passenger side. No keys. *Wait a minute. If this is an Agency vehicle, Cate should have stashed a master in her pack.* Hope felt the compartments. *Aha!* She pulled the key fob, and the lock clicked. She opened the door and slipped inside, starting the truck as she slid across the bench seat. The seat sat high. Hope could barely touch the pedals or see over the dash, but she could drive standing if need be.

Laughing merrily, she hit the gas and attempted to speed away, but the truck immediately stalled. The horn began to blare. Dammit, it *was* a trap! Hope jumped out of the truck and crashed back into the forest. She could hear people yelling, no longer concerned about being stealthy. No, they were letting her know that they had their prey in sight. *Do the unexpected girl, do the unexpected.*

Hope stopped. She watched as people dressed in camouflage raced from the trees toward the truck. Instead of running away, she scrambled behind a large tree and waited. Someone silenced the horn, then shut off the truck. They searched the area, and upon finding the com she had discarded on the other side of the road, decided she had run back into the forest.

Hope waited until the searchers dispersed. She crawled under the truck, near a large wheel. If they came back, she could either hide in the wheel well or roll out into a ditch. For now, she'd just wait until the sun went down. It would take them some time to find Cate, but once they found her and realized Hope had swiped her phone, they would try to track her. Hope pulled the phone from her pack, extracted the SIM card and wrapped it in the foil wrapper from her protein bar. She had learned much from the bodyguards who had protected her in her youth, in particular, that foil deflected tracking signals. She would need the card and the phone later, but by then, she would be long gone.

Hope smiled at the hotel clerk. An old trucker had picked her up on Highway Seven and dropped her off at a popular hotel chain near Leesburg, VA.

"Hi, I was hiking in Bears Den Park and ran into some trouble with a bear." She smirked. "Damn thing started chasing me. I barely managed to get away. Ran all the way to the highway. Unfortunately, my car was in the opposite direction. Hitched a ride from a trucker on Highway Seven. I'm going to need a room. I'll arrange to get back there tomorrow. Right now, all I want is a hot shower, a good meal, and a soft bed to sleep in."

The hotel clerk studied her. She frowned at Hope's scratched up limbs and dirty clothes. "Damn, girl. You look like you're worse for wear. Are you sure you don't need a hospital?"

Hope shook her head. "A hot shower will clean me up and I'll be fine."

The clerk's eyes rounded. "You are pretty dirty. You might want a change of clothes, too. We've got a shop that sells tee shirts and things. Would that help?"

Hope grinned. "Definitely."

The clerk smiled and handed her a form. "Well, fill this out, give me a credit card, and you're in business."

Hope quickly filled out the form and handed it back to the clerk. She held up Cate's phone and pointed at the screen. "I assume you take this bank app?"

The clerk nodded. "Sure do. Just swipe it and we're done." She pointed to a hallway off to the side of the front desk. "The store is right around the corner. It should have everything you need. Your room is on the fourth floor. You can get pizza delivery or room service for thirty more minutes. You'd better hurry if you want food."

"Where the hell is she?" Cade glared at Dianna, Anders, Tom, and Cate. "She's been gone for more than sixteen hours. Carmichael lost her. You lost her. For some reason, we can't track her medical chip. What the hell did she do? Wrap herself in aluminum foil? Now we don't know where the hell she is. She could be in danger. She could be hurt. She could be dead. I cannot believe that with all the technology we have at our fingertips, you lost her." He frowned.

Tom snorted. "Hell, I wouldn't put it past Hope to hop a plane and head back to Wisconsin just to make us sweat."

Dianna shrugged. "I already called. She's not there."

Cade looked to each person in turn. "Well, any other ideas?"

"Knowing Hope, she's sitting in a café somewhere, refueling." Tom tried not to smile. "That teeny tiny woman eats more than me."

Cate nodded. "And I wouldn't put it past her to buy new clothes and find a hotel room to clean up in." Her eyes lit up. "In fact, even though she wasn't carrying a credit card, Hope has all her account numbers memorized. I've heard her rattle one off when she didn't have her card with her."

Anders ran a hand through his hair. "Do we have those numbers anywhere?"

Cade shook his head. "No, but I bet her parents do. God, I am going to get a lot of shit for calling them and asking."

Dianna snapped her fingers. "Wait. Janet can find them. She can also find out if Hope used one of her cards recently. She was just showing me how to hack into the records of un-cooperative credit card companies."

Cade pulled a phone from his pocket and hit a button. "Let's hope Janet's not teaching a class. She gets pissed when I interrupt her." He listened, then spoke into the phone. "Hey, hon. We need a favor. When you get this, can you hack into whatever and find Hope's credit card accounts, then see if she used any of them today? She managed to evade the rest of the team on her field test, and well, now we can't find her." He laughed. "And before you say it, yes, I know, we should have expected this to happen." He disconnected.

Tom frowned. "So now we wait?"

Cade nodded. "Unless you have a better idea, we wait. I'll take the couch. You guys get the chairs. The whole point of the field test is to prove you can break out of captivity and if possible, return to base or call for help. There's a special bonus for breaking out and evading recapture for twenty-four hours, but most don't go for that. Most want to get back to a warm bed. Staying away is so Hope's style. My only objective is to ensure that she has a clear path back. If Janet does find her, all we can do is observe and follow unless some other form of intervention is warranted. Understood?"

Everyone in the group nodded.

Cade smirked. "And just maybe we'll learn something from this."

The next morning, Hope slipped into a rental car and adjusted the seat. Not high enough. She stepped out of the car, grabbed the bag of dirty clothes she had stashed in the back seat and placed it on the driver's seat, then sat on top of it. Better. At least now she could reach the pedals *and* see out the windshield.

Her own car had a four-inch seat cushion. Maybe she should have asked for one from the rental agency. At just five feet, she was tall enough to ride a rollercoaster, but most other things were just a little too high or a little too big or a little too wide. While she had learned to adapt, when she was without her assistive tools—seat cushions, high-heeled shoes, grabbers, and the like—she was like a fish without fins. Unable to swim in the shark pool.

Hope started the car and plugged in the address of the camp. "Travel time, two hours and three minutes," the GPS announced. Then it began to give her instructions to the nearest freeway.

Hope glanced at the clock on the dashboard. She had managed to evade capture for more than twenty-four hours. All she had to do was get back and report in. Hope smirked. *Piece of cake.* She pulled into a fast-food restaurant that appeared on the side of the road and ordered a large cup of coffee and a sweet roll. After taking a few sips of coffee, she pulled back onto the road and headed south.

Two and a half hours later, Hope pulled up to the gate of the Agency compound and waved at the guard. "Hey, Henderson. I'm reporting back from my field exercise."

Henderson scowled. "I.D.?"

"Henderson, they kidnapped me and stripped me of everything, including my I.D. You know that and you know who I am. Let me in."

Henderson shook his head. "Against protocol. I'll have to call for someone to come down and identify you." He smiled slightly. "Sorry, them's the rules. Even for you. And just for the record, I lost twenty bucks in the pool. You snookered everyone."

Hope grinned. "I'll buy you a beer the next time I see you out and about."

Henderson nodded. "I'll hold you to that."

Anders jogged up to the gate, a big smile on his face. He pounded on the hood of Hope's car. "The prodigal child returns!" He smacked Henderson on the arm. "I'm surprised she's not wearing her Wonder Woman uniform."

Hope blushed. "Oh, pul-eeze. I just did what I do best. Left all of you old folks in the dust." She cackled. "All that matters is that I passed. Next stop, graduation." She pumped her fist. "Woo-hoo!"

Henderson raised the gate and with a sweeping motion, gestured for her to pass. Hope hit the gas and drove to the main office, leaving Anders behind her. She could hear him shouting. *Gee, I hope he didn't expect me to give him a ride. No sense in giving him one last opportunity to derail this gig.* After she parked the car, Hope grabbed her bag of clothing and strolled to Cade's office. She knocked and poked her head in the door. "Looking for me, boss?" She grinned. "I'm baaaack."

Cade looked up from his computer, and a puzzled look

crossed his face. "Where's Tom and Cate? They should have been right behind you."

Hope flapped her hand. "Oh, once I spotted them, I led them on a merry chase. Lost them in a drive-through about ten miles out. Then I took a side road in. They never caught up." She smirked. "I think the lady behind me was ordering for a family of ten. They had a long wait in a well-contained line. No way they could have followed me without breaking through a barrier wall about four feet high."

Cade winced. "You tunneled them?"

Hope shrugged. "It was an old drive-through. No way to pull out of the line once you were in it, and since the exit leads directly back onto the street, there was no way for someone else to go around and cut someone else off. Guess they've never been there before." She grinned. "So, did I pass?"

Cade threw down his pencil. "Of course, you did. There was never any doubt. You ruffled Cate and Carmichael's feathers for taking them down, though. And Cate's pissed that you used her credit card. You racked up some nice charges out there." He smirked. "A mani-pedi? Really?"

Hope flashed her well-manicured hands at him. "My hands got a little torn up when I was running through the woods."

Cade stared at her nails. "Is that Wonder Woman painted on your thumbnails?"

Hope shrugged. Her face started to turn red. Then she giggled. "It's just a joke. *I know* I'm not Wonder Woman. But if others want to worship at that altar, who am I to complain?

He chuckled. "Well, be prepared for a flood of Wonder Woman shit now—hats, tee shirts, lingerie. People around here don't let go of stuff that easily. You may rue the day you embraced that tag." Cade smirked. "Anyway, you're going to have to make nice with Cate and Carmichael. The rest of the gang is going to be giving them shit for a while. Cate will laugh it off. She doesn't care. Much. Carmichael holds a grudge. And you might need him out in the field. Kiss and make up, okay?"

Hope nodded. "I'll try. Even *I* know you get more flies with honey than vinegar."

Cade snorted. "Not sure Carmichael would appreciate being called a fly."

Hope cocked her head. "Well, he was being a pest with that drone."

"As assigned."

"Next time, tell him not to wear fluorescent hunter's orange. He was too easy to spot in the trees."

Cade sighed. "*Most* would have been too frazzled to notice. *Most* don't hang around — they run for the hills the minute they escape. *You* did the unexpected." He patted himself on the back. "I taught you well."

Hope scrunched up her face. "No, Hazelton did." She giggled. "You just cleaned up the rough edges."

Cade rolled his eyes and snorted. "What's important is what you've become, and that's one damn fine agent. A few inches taller and a hundred pounds heavier, and you could be the best one ever."

Hope smiled. "Oh, you ain't seen nothing yet."

CHAPTER SIX: THE ASSIGNMENT

Cade swiped the console, and a photo of a beautiful dark-haired young woman appeared on the whiteboard.

The set of her thick red lips hinted at a stern demeanor, but her large brown eyes, framed in kohl, were filled with humor. "This is Alya Nahar. Age twenty-two. Five feet tall. Approximately ninety-eight pounds. She has just completed an expose on some of the most prominent families in the United Arab Emirates." He stopped talking and took a sip from a coffee mug. "The good, the bad, the ugly. The down dirty and nasty. It's claimed she possesses information on some of most horrendous skeletons in the six royal families' closets.

"Three weeks ago, she was snatched off the streets of Cardiff, Wales, where she has been in hiding. Coincidentally, that was just one week after her agent began shopping her book to publishers all over the world. There is a bidding war going on."

"Do we know where she is?" Anders frowned. "Is she still alive?"

"We believe she has entered the ranks of the *enforced disappeared*, but yes, by all accounts, she is still alive."

A puzzled look crossed Tom's face. "The what?"

Cade again swiped at the console and a map of the Middle East appeared on the whiteboard. "*Enforced disappeared* refers to people abducted or imprisoned by state or political organizations. In the past forty years, the U.N. has documented more than fifty-five thousand cases of enforced disappearances worldwide. Bahrain, Egypt, Saudi Arabia, and the UAE are among those countries with misplaced citizens.

"In most cases, after a country snatches a person, they decline to disclose their fate. Most won't even admit to their existence. Some go to prison and are left to rot, while others — ranking government officials, prominent businesspeople, and even princes — are held under house arrest. Often, they are detained in luxurious accommodations but kept under heavy guard. They are not permitted to leave their residence, but some are allowed visitors."

Cade swiped at the console and a photo of Alya in an abaya and hijab — the full-length gown and head-covering common for women in Muslim communities — appeared. "This photo was taken surreptitiously by Alya's father, who was permitted to visit. His stated purpose was to convince her to withdraw her book from publication. Instead, he managed to smuggle out this photo." He gestured at the whiteboard. "Obviously, she's alive. Her father confirmed that this is, in fact, his daughter."

Hope frowned. "Why do we care? She's not an American. I thought we didn't interfere unless an American was involved." Hope tried to contain her excitement. She had completed her first assignment easily. It had been a simple drop near the Russian border. Now she was ready for something a little more exciting.

Cade nodded. "That's true. However, this book could confirm some long-held rumors about the role Middle Eastern countries and their royal families have played in supporting terrorism, not only in the U.S. but around the world. Financial support, safe havens, disinformation fed to law enforcement, all sorts of details we've never been able to verify. Apparently, Nahar has collected witness testimony, financial documents, surveillance videos, everything we need to shut financial and arms pipelines down." He studied the woman's photo and said slowly, "Even if she doesn't manage to get this information into print, we want the manuscript and the documents that back up her claims."

"What's the problem?" Anders asked. "Surely her agent —
"

Cade shook his head. "Not that easy. The agent doesn't have the book. She only has a synopsis — a proposal. That doesn't include any specific details."

Cate asked, "So where's the book?"

"On a flash drive in a Swiss Bank that only Nahar can access, in person. A retina scan and thumbprint are required. The Swiss don't mess around. They won't let anyone but Nahar claim it, and only then if she appears willingly." Cade steepled his fingers and studied the faces of his agents. "Look, our government wants that information. The President believes that we are the only ones who should have it. Any other country would use it for blackmail or other illicit purposes. We really don't have a stake in the game other than as targets and unwitting Allies. We have clean hands, but some other countries may not. The President wants to know if any of our foreign aid or arms trades are somehow being funneled into the hands of terrorists. The people who receive that aid certainly aren't going to tell us." He shook his head. "In the past year, a lot of questions have been raised about the true allegiance of certain Middle Eastern countries. This is just one piece of the puzzle, but a very important one."

Cate also steepled her fingers and rested her head on them. "Are we even sure she has the information? Has anyone actually seen it? I mean, she's twenty-two. How could she even access that type of information? This could be one big set-up. A way to make America look bad, again."

Cade swiped at the console and a large group photo of men dressed in thawbs appeared. "There are seven emirates in the UAE. They are ruled by six royal families. The personalities of the leaders of those royal families is mixed. Some have pushed hard for gender equality and have actually made great strides. Women are assuming a more significant role in the workforce and the government. In addition, they are no longer denied an education. Over two-thirds of college graduates in the UAE are women, including Nahar. She attended the Women's College, where it is believed she mingled freely with and befriended many younger members of the royal families. There is no way to determine who her sources are, but given the access she had, there is every reason to believe her claims are legitimate."

Tom frowned. "If they are so liberal, so supportive of gender equality, why is Nahar under house arrest?"

Cade studied him. "Because it is believed she possesses and is about to expose what some consider their dirty laundry. Some families are actively involved in terrorism and some have merely looked the other way. The royal families in the UAE make every effort to appear to be friendly to the U.S., but the reality is, some are wolves in sheep's clothing. They play both sides of the fence. They may need us, but that doesn't mean they actually support us. Nahar threatens their relationship with the U.S. and other countries in Europe. Depending on what information she has, all hell could break loose. Their relationship with us could be damaged, permanently."

"What are the chances the country will clean house on their own, just on the threat of exposure?" Anders asked.

Cade smirked. "Much easier to quash the book and its author, don't you think?"

Hope nodded. "Freedom of speech is a different concept to them, as in, it doesn't exist. We need to look at this through their lens, not ours. Many will feel the royal families are justified in detaining Nahar. Others may not like her house arrest but are unwilling to sacrifice themselves or their families to publicly fight it. The risks to Nahar and her family are very real." She gazed at Cade. "Our interference is neither welcome or wise. We will still be seen as *Infidels*. That's a wealthy country. We don't give them much financial aid. We pretty much provide military support, which they could also get from Russia." Hope shook her head. "If they hate us now, our interference may cause them to hate us even more. This seems counterproductive."

Cade switched the whiteboard back to the complete photo of Alya Nahar. "That doesn't alter our predicament, though. This is information we need, and this may be the best way to get it. This isn't just about the security of our country. It concerns the security of the free world. We need to know who our true enemies are." He sighed. "As for Nahar, the U.N. considers *the disappeared* a global problem. They have a vested interest in the rescue of Nahar and exposing the circumstances behind her disappearance. This is a humanitarian mission with political overtones and we are the only ones with the authority to pull it off."

Cate gazed at Cade. "Why not seek a diplomatic solution? Ask for Nahar in exchange for our silence about her abduction? Or maybe offer an exchange for someone from Gitmo?" She snorted. "It's not like that hasn't happened before."

"Already tried that. They won't even admit they have her. If it wasn't for her literary agent, *we* wouldn't even know she had been taken or the information she possesses."

Hope sighed. "So, if we remove her from her prison, there will be no outcry? No retaliation? I think you'd better talk to my parents. They'll shatter those rose-colored glasses."

Cade smiled. "Already on their way. We'll be working with them. They know people. We'll supply the muscle and the brains. They'll grease the skids, so to speak. We may not need to get involved at all, just pick her up at the border."

Hope groaned. "I aced agent training for this? Seems to me I earned the chance to prove myself outside my parent's shadow. This is almost embarrassing."

Tom chuckled. *"Spycraft One Zero Two*, princess. Find the best source of information and milk it for all its worth. Who's the best source of information here?"

Hope's sigh was begrudging. "My parents."

Anders nodded. "Bingo."

Marianne Benson glared at her husband, Sheikh Harun Ali. "I don't care what you agreed to. Hope is going to resent the hell out of this. She's going to think we're interfering."

"How can we be interfering when we are their best re-source? Besides, we're ensuring her safety. We're reducing the risk to her life. You know Cade is going to send her in there. He has to. You saw that photo of Alya Nahar. She and Hope could be sisters, if not twins. Add a little makeup and Hope's her clone. Cade is going to try to pull a switch or use her to confuse Nahar's captors. The man is too crafty not to. How can we sit on our hands? Especially when we could do something that would guarantee a better outcome?"

Mari closed her eyes and pursed her lips. *Fathers. How can I make him see?* Mari sighed deeply and said, "Look at it from her perspective. She has something to prove. She doesn't need Daddy smoothing the way."

Harun frowned. His elegant British accent grew clipped. "I'm not going in the field with her and holding her hand, dear. I am merely going to try to figure out a way to get access with the least amount of fallout. Money talks over there. And I know who can be bought."

Mari sighed. "Well, you are a sneaky devil. Hope does get that from you. But I don't want her to feel like we are smoth-ering her, either. We need to keep it professional and not be her parents, but colleagues. Understood?"

Harun snorted. "Says the mother who still sends her care

packages."

Mari blushed. "A little reminder that you are loved and missed never hurts. I did that for all my children." She paused. "About this book . . . What could the author possibly have that we don't? Our database is pretty extensive. It's hard to believe that she found something we missed."

"No idea. We have nailed down the major financial connections for most of the terrorist groups. We know where the money is coming from. However, she may have been close enough to the royals to report conversations or witness transactions. That may be useful as well. And remember, I follow the money trail. I have no strong sense of the relationships and connections that lead to the money or an association with a terrorist cell. She could be coming at it from a whole different angle."

Harun came up behind Mari and kissed her neck, then ran a hand down her arm. He cupped her breast and squeezed. Mari moaned as he pulled her blouse from her yoga pants and reached underneath. His hand skimmed her stomach and his hand dipped beneath her panties. His fingers stroked her mound and slipped inside of her. "So wet, wife," he crooned.

"Harun, what are you doing?"

Harun grinned wickedly. "Seducing my wife. Our nest is empty. I can take my wife anywhere in this big old house without interruption." He pulled her over to a table in the kitchen and pushed her down on her back. He pulled at her top and lifted it up to her shoulders. "And the fact my wife isn't wearing a bra tells me she is unlikely to refuse."

Mari gazed at him and smiled. Her voice was low and husky when she said, "And when have I ever refused you, dear? You know I love you madly, even when you do try to take over Hope's life."

Harun unsnapped his jeans and slowly pulled down the zipper.

Mari giggled. "And who's going commando this morning, darling?"

Harun smiled, kicked off his shoes, and tossed the jeans aside. "I think we had the same idea. Maybe we should just run around naked. It would be more expedient." He reached for Mari and tore her pants and panties from her body.

Mari tossed her shirt to the floor at the same time as Harun did his. He slid Mari to the end of the table and grabbed her legs by the ankle, pulling them over his shoulders. He grabbed his rigid cock and began to rub her center.

Mari's eyes held his as he slid inside her, gently at first, then he began to thrust hard, bucking against Mari, pulling her hips toward him as he speared her. Mary felt that curdle of heat rise from her core, the flames dancing to the end of her fingertips and toes. *God, I love this man.* And she loved the way he made her feel. She arched her back as her head filled with vivid colors. Mari gasped and her body began to tremble. Then she let go. As she slipped off the cliff of ecstasy, she clutched at her husband.

Harun groaned as her vagina gripped him and he bellowed her name as he filled her. Then he collapsed on top of her, kissing Mari deeply. "I love you, wife," he whispered. "Mine."

Tom wrapped his arm around Hope as they watched the Baltimore Ravens take on the Green Bay Packers. "You know I'm a *Cowboys,* fan, right? The only reason I'm watching the Packers is that the *Cowboys* play Monday night." He pulled at a strand of her long black hair. "And you asked me nicely."

Hope laughed. "Don't say that to my father. He has learned to love the Packers in the six years we've lived in the States. My mom would kick him out of the house if he cheered for anyone else." She grabbed onto Tom's shaggy dark hair and kissed him. "Besides, they have season tickets. When we visit, we'll be going to Lambeau Field for the games." She giggled. "And we will freeze our asses off."

Tom smiled. "Well, that's what beer is for."

Hope grinned. "You might want to warm it up on the grill when we're tailgating, though." She smirked. "Unless you're going to be a wuss and insist on sitting in the car to stay warm. I know you southern boys get cold easily. Heck, when we play the Cowboys at home, they look like they're freezing their little willies off."

"Hope, I've been living in the D.C. area for a few years now. I know how to stay warm."

Hope burst out laughing. "My God, they shut down everything when it snows around here. The roads are empty, grocery store shelves are bare, people stay in their homes until it melts. They have never seen a *real* winter. And I doubt they could survive it. My parents live on a farm in central Wisconsin. It gets so cold, cow poop freezes before it hits the ground. Sometimes, the snow is so deep, we can't get out to the main roads for days. We have to use snowshoes to get the mail. And they never cancel school, because school bus drivers are fearless. If the bus starts, they hit the road and we are forced to bundle up, trudge through the snow, and get on that bus and get to school. In Wisconsin, snow stops no one.

"So, we will be out there cheering the Packers no matter the weather. Sure, we have hand warmers stuffed everywhere and flasks of brandy in our coats, but nothing keeps us from cheering on our team."

Tom pulled Hope on his lap and began to kiss her. His hand roamed and he slowly inched up her sweater. "Nothing, Hope. Not even this?"

Hope slapped at his hand. "Keep your hands to yourself, Buster. I'm watching the game." She sighed. "Some of those players fill out those uniforms quite nicely. Look at those exquisite arses." She turned away from him, her eyes fixed on the television.

Tom groaned and began to kiss her neck. "I think you need to learn to multi-task, Hope. I hear some females are really good at it."

"Sexist pig," she muttered. Hope bent her head further, allowing him more access, but her eyes remained focused on the TV. Tom's hand returned to the bottom of her sweater and began to pull it up. Hope emitted an exasperated sigh and pulled her sweater off, tossing it to the side.

Tom's hands began to knead her breasts.

Hope moaned, but her attention was still on the game.

Tom tugged at her bra.

Hope removed it, saying nothing.

Tom laid her back on the sofa and covered Hope with his body. He nibbled on her neck, moved to her breasts, sucked at her nipples, then moved further down past her stomach.

Hope sighed, but her head remained turned toward the TV. Suddenly she flew off the sofa, knocking Tom off to the side. She screamed excitedly and jumped up and down. "Touchdown!" she yelled. She turned to Tom, a big smile on her face.

Tom stared at her, then he laughed, throwing his head back as he roared.

Hope planted her hands on her hips and scowled. "Are you laughing at my half-naked body?"

Tom pulled her back on his lap and began stroke her again. "I was trying to play with you, and you didn't even notice. Your attention was solely on the TV and football tail. What's wrong with this picture?"

Hope cuddled into him and laced her hands around his neck. She kissed him. "Well, then, I guess you just have to try harder."

Hope awoke the next morning and sat up quickly, breaking away from Tom's embrace.

He rolled onto his back and moaned. "Dammit, Hope. You almost knocked me in the eye."

She grinned down at him and kissed his forehead. Cheerfully, she said, "Oh, wake up, you big fat grouch. I slept like a rock and I'm hungry."

"Of course, you are," Tom groaned. "But first, we have a little business to attend to." He grabbed her hand and placed it on his stiff penis.

Hope crooned, "Oh, Tommy, darling. Is that for me?"

"I don't see anyone else waiting around for it. So, yes, it's for you." He sat up and swung his legs over the side of the bed, fisting his cock, stroking its length.

Hope dropped to her knees and reached for it. She smiled and ran her tongue across her lips. "I want to taste your pretty cock." Hope grasped it at the base, stuck out her tongue, and began to lick, running her tongue up and down its length. Her tongue swirled around the tip and she moaned as she tasted Tom's pre-cum. *So good.*

Tom grabbed her long hair and twisted it in his fist, pulling her more tightly against him. Softly, he said, "Open, Hope. Take me in."

God, I love it when he exerts his dominance, pulling on my hair. Hope leaned back and her eyes locked with his. She opened her mouth and allowed him to push his rock-hard penis in. As his member slid over her tongue and toward her throat, Hope began to hum. The vibrations made his cock become stiffer, fuller.

Tom groaned and forcefully stroked his cock through her lips, pushing deeper and deeper.

Hope leaned back and opened her throat, trying not to gag. She loved the feel of Tom's cock down her throat, the knowledge that only she had the power to bring him to such heights. It was pure feminine power. She reached for his balls and gently caressed them.

Tom continued to fuck her throat, his movements more distracted now. He pulled at her hair again and primal noises emerged from his lips. Suddenly, he yanked her hair hard and slammed his cock the rest of the way down her throat. Then he shuddered and yelled her name.

Tom exploded inside her mouth and Hope hungrily drank as the semen flowed. When Tom finished, she swallowed and licked her lips. She rose to her feet and kissed him deeply. Then she giggled. "Still hungry, darling. I want waffles, bacon, and eggs."

Hope sat at the kitchen table wearing Tom's tee shirt. She said nothing as she shoveled in a waffle topped with bacon, an egg with a leaky yolk, and a heavy dose of butter and syrup.

Tom shook his head. "How can you eat that? It's disgusting. Not to mention artery-blocking, fat-enhancing, and just plain unhealthy."

Hope pointed her fork at him. "Do I criticize you when you suck down oysters loaded with hot sauce, horseradish, and mustard? *That's* disgusting. You don't even chew. You just swallow. You have whole oysters rotting in your stomach. They can't even pass until they fully decompose. Food is meant to be thoroughly chewed so it passes smoothly through your digestive tract. When you die and they open you up, your stomach will reek because it's become a composter." She picked up another piece of waffle and delicately added a forkful of egg and bacon. "This is a little piece of heaven. I can taste every little morsel of goodness. It gives me pleasure." She smiled wickedly. "*The greatest pleasure of all.*"

Tom sighed and shook his head. "I know full well sex is at the top of your list, despite your claims to the contrary. But for such a teeny, tiny human, you sure seem to require a lot of sugar and fat. I don't get it. Last night, your steak was bigger than mine and you ate it in half the time. You inhale food."

Hope smirked and tapped her head. "And I burn it off, equally fast. Brain food, sir. Keeps my mind well-tuned and limber."

Tom laughed. "If you say so." He dipped his toast into some egg yolk and took a bite.

Hope shook her head. "And that, sir, is disgusting. Who dips their toast in egg yolk, like it's some kind of dip or something? Put the damn egg on the toast and cut it into bite-size pieces." She sighed. "I guess that's to be expected of Texas boys. Ya'll think biscuits and gravy, mustard grits, and country fried steak are the best way to start the day. *Yuck!*"

The buzzer for Hope's apartment door sounded. She frowned. "Who could that be?" She rose from the table and walked to the door, gazing through the peephole. Hope gasped. "Oh my God, it's my parents. Quick. Hide!"

Tom glared. "Not happening. We're adults. We're allowed to engage in adult relationships. I am not hiding from your parents."

Hope crossed her arms and glared back. She hissed, "You're wearing nothing but your boxers. My parents will *not* meet you in your boxers."

Tom gazed at his lap and hastily stood. "Yeah, that might be a deal breaker." He hurried from the room.

The buzzer sounded again and Hope swung open the door. "Mom. Dad. What brings you here?"

Her father peered over her shoulder and grinned. "Are we interrupting something, my darling daughter?"

Her mother nudged him and said in a soft voice, "I told you we should have called first. She has company." Mari tugged at his sleeve. "Let's give her a chance to get herself together and come back, later. *Much later.*"

Hope nodded. "Good idea—no, *great* idea. Later. Much

later." Hope tried to close the door, but her father blocked it.

"Oh, nonsense. Now is as good of a time as ever to meet the man warming your bed." Harun swept past her into the apartment. He studied the food on the kitchen table and turned to Hope. Harun cocked an eyebrow. "Unless you're going to claim you're eating for two?"

"No, I—" Hope sputtered.

Tom walked into the foyer, dressed only in jeans, and stuck out his hand. "Good to see you again, sir." He glanced down at his bare chest. "Sorry for the semi-nudity, but Hope seems to be wearing my shirt."

Harun smacked him on the shoulder, then shook his hand. He laughed. "What's a little nudity amongst family, Tom?"

Hope's eyes narrowed, her gaze darting between the two men. Through gritted teeth, she asked, "You two know each other?" She smacked Tom on the same shoulder. "You met my father and didn't tell me?"

Tom rubbed his shoulder and frowned. "God, woman. That was more than a playful tap." He nodded at her father. "Remember when Rami snatched you? Your father was on the first plane out, making sure Rami didn't spirit you out of the country."

Hope's mouth formed into an O, but she said nothing.

Harun continued, "And while we were searching for you, your man and I had quite a heart to heart."

Hope frowned. "You did?" She cocked her head. "About what?"

Tom cleared his throat. "What do you think a father says to the man who professes his love for his precious and only daughter?"

Hope paled. "What?"

"Darn it, Hope. I didn't know where you were, whether you were dead or alive. Whether I would ever see you again. Rami was a loose cannon. I didn't know what he was capable of. I kinda went off the rails. So yeah, I told him I loved you."

Harun nodded. "And of all the agents looking for you, he was the one truly rattled." He chuckled. "He was panicked. Then Cade booted him out of the room and told him to get his act together." He shrugged. "I was curious, so I followed. Spilled his guts before he could introduce himself."

"Excuse me. May I join this party?" Mari moved through the doorway and extended her arm toward Tom. "Hi, Tom. I've heard all about you. Even read your file." At Tom's startled expression, she smirked. "You didn't think my husband would let you date his daughter without running a complete background check, did you? I know more about you than I ever wanted to." She waved toward his well-defined chest. "Though this is impressive."

Hope groaned and sunk to the floor. She buried her head in her hands. "This is so embarrassing."

Tom, Harun, and Mari all laughed.

Finally, Harun said, "Well, my sweet daughter. Perhaps you should have introduced us to Tom, instead of trying to hide him."

Hope spread the fingers of one hand and peered up at her father. "I wasn't trying to hide anything, Dad. I'm an adult now. I don't have to share every little detail with you."

Mari grinned. "She's right, you know. Her business is her business unless she chooses to share it. Face it, darling, your little bird has flown the nest and she's got her own life now. I would have been horrified if my father had stuck his nose into my love life."

"Thanks, Mom," Hope murmured.

Mari tugged at her husband's arm. "Now let's go check into our hotel." She smiled at Tom. "Perhaps we can meet later, say dinner at seven?"

Tom knelt next to Hope. "Hon? Seven, okay?"

Hope nodded.

Mari grinned. "I think I like you, Tom. You let Hope decide for herself instead of assuming it was okay." She kissed her husband on the cheek. "Something my husband does well when he isn't distracted. Let's go check into our hotel and take a nap." She winked at Hope. "You know how your father adores naps."

Hope shook her head and groaned. "Oh, I so did not need to hear that!"

CHAPTER SEVEN: THE PLAN

Cade studied the people gathered in the conference room. It was time to plan.

He put down the donut he had snatched out of the bag in the middle of the table and nodded at the photos posted on the whiteboard. One photo was of the target, Alya Nahar. Another was a photo of Hope. The third was a photo of Hope made up like Nahar — eyes rimmed in charcoal and lips outlined in blood red. "Obviously, we need to decide how to best use Hope. She's practically a dead ringer for Nahar. Her height. Her weight. Her face. Add a little makeup and she could be Nahar."

Harun cocked an eyebrow. "If you send her into the UAE, can you keep her safe?"

Hope opened her mouth to speak, but Cade waved her off. He glared at Harun. "You may be my best friend, but that was just plain insulting. Hope is a fully trained agent. She excelled at every task she was given. I would not send her into the Middle East if I did not think she was ready. And she will not be alone. She will have backup. I have never, ever left an agent behind. You *know* that."

Mari cleared her throat. "Ignore my husband. He is having a little trouble letting our youngest go, even though she is old enough to be married and have children.

Harun flushed, and Mari laughed. She turned to the whiteboard. "What about a play on three-card Monty? If we can find someone else who closely resembles Nahar, we could create a train of confusion. Spread them out, confuse any watchers."

Cate nodded. "We could use makeup, a pair of brown contacts, an abaya and hijab, but we would need a very similar body type. We're talking a small woman, here. Do we even have anyone who fits, other than Hope?"

Cade shook his head. "Not in our Agency. We may have to take someone from one of the lettered agencies on loan. But that involves a lot of paperwork and exposing our plans to a greater number of people, which in turn increases the likelihood of a leak. Once you bring in other agencies, you also have to deal with conflicting agendas. And we won't know what those agendas are until the harm is done. That's why we keep our assignments so contained. The fewer who know what we're up to, the better."

Tom leaned forward, his hands wrapped around a coffee mug. "So how do we use Hope, then? Do we make a switch? Use Hope as a distraction? Or do we not use her at all?"

Harun nodded. "Maybe there is a legitimate way to get Nahar out of her rooms and grab her then."

Cade smirked. "You mean like bringing in an exterminator?"

Harun smiled. "Why not? Rats and mice are common in those areas, as are almost any type of household pest — ants, bed bugs, wasps. Hell, we could create our own infestation. Just put a word in the right ear and we could get the place shut down."

"What other reason could we use to force an evacuation of the building where she's being held?"

Tom cocked his head. "A bomb threat?'

"Gas? Or a strong order, like sulfur?" Anders studied the donut he had pulled out of the bakery bag and took a small bite. "Heck, throw cherry bombs down a few toilets and you could totally fuck up the plumbing."

Cate laughed. "So that was you in my dormitory?" She

grinned. "And they blamed *me*."

Cade made a circular motion with his hand. "Keep going. We need something that won't create suspicion but will have the desired result. We need to get her out of her apartment, to the airport, and on a plane."

Tom's eyes narrowed. "We could just put sleeping gas in her air vents and knock everyone out, swoop in and take her."

Mari tapped her finger on the table. "What do we know about the building she's held in? Are others who disappeared held there? And if so, are they each assigned their own guards or is there a general security force? If it's just her and a few guards, we could use that Chinese doping spray Janet always talks about. Walk up to the guards, one squirt and they're out. Because if she is the only one there, who's going to notice a few men slumped on the floor? People will assume they're drunk."

Cade gestured at Harun. "Let's see what the Sheikh can find out, and, if need be, one of us can go in and look around to confirm. I like the idea of some sort of evacuation. Getting her out of the building completely before we grab her, but it will have to be planned to the last detail, which means we have to be sure of all the moving parts. Not only do we have to know about the guard detail, but we also need to know if there is some sort of evacuation plan already in place. They may have instructions to toss her in a van and take her elsewhere if something unexpected happens."

Hope's eyes narrowed. "What if their evacuation plan is to just shoot the prisoner and run?"

Harun nodded. "That is not outside the realm of possibility. If they are using men who are not professionals, they are more likely to panic and do something stupid. However, whoever took her wants something. Her book. Perhaps they would be more likely to protect her until they get what they want."

Tom frowned. "Do we know if anyone else is looking for her? The Brits, for example? She was hiding out in Wales. Surely they knew she was there. And surely they've noticed she's gone. That could be a big complication. It's not like they haven't interfered before. MISix has injected themselves into more than one of our operations, and without notice. It would be just like those assholes to swoop in and scoop up the target after we've rescued her."

Harun nodded. "He has a point. The information contained in Alya's book could just as easily concern the Brits. That may be why they offered her shelter. And if the information concerns a botched operation or exposes one of their agents, they may have lost her and now want her back." He ran a hand through his hair. "Hope may even come face-to-face with her Uncle Abdul. This is just the type of scenario he thrives on. And he would undercut Hope without a thought, even if she is his flesh and blood. We're still not sure where his loyalties lie after the terrorists claimed he was in on the plot to make those planes disappear. They said he wanted us dead."

Mari placed a hand on his arm. "Honey, your brother gave *us* no evidence of duplicity. I suspect the terrorists were just blowing smoke. Besides, if he really wanted us dead, he had plenty of opportunities. He wasn't at our home long, but long enough to kill us if that was his plan."

Hope paled. "You thought Uncle Abdul wanted us dead? No." She shook her head. "No. That's just wrong. He wouldn't—"

Cade held up a hand. "Nonetheless, in an operation like this, no one is an ally unless I tell you they're an ally. Trust no one but the people in this room."

Harun cleared his throat. "There are, of course, other concerns about sending Hope to the Middle East. Some members of the royal families in the UAE are closely aligned with families in Saudi Arabia, including my own. And we don't know whether their allegiance lies with those who put a price our heads."

Hope nodded. "I have six brothers. They are spread out around the world. I haven't seen any of them since we sought asylum in the U.S., but one lives in France, two in England, and one in Singapore. Only two, Khalid and Mehdi, live in the Middle East." She cocked her head. "Are those two still a concern, even after the death of my grandfather?"

Harun gazed at Mari, his eyes raised in question. Mari shifted uncomfortably in her seat, then spoke. "It appears your brother, Khalid, played a role in brokering the marriage contract with Rami. Although that contract was canceled and Rami is still in jail waiting for trial on your kidnapping, your brother seems to have taken an interest in your whereabouts. He has been asking questions."

"Questions? Why? The contract is null and void. Rami is essentially *persona non grata* in Saudi Arabia. Why would my brother continue to have an interest?"

Harun said, "We believe that to him it is a matter of honor. He brokered the contract, and he is furious that it was nullified by outside parties."

Hope shook her head. "No. It was nullified by you, his father. You had every right to nullify it. He had no right to agree to it in the first place."

"Sharia Law, Hope. He was sanctioned by your grandfather who, some believe, had every right to arrange your marriage. The fact that I rejected the Muslim faith and became a Christian, and the fact that your mother is an Infidel . . ."

Cade nodded. "And the fact that your parents not only seek prosecution of terrorists and then bankrupt them, some of whom were linked to your grandfather . . ."

Harun gazed at Hope. "They have some convinced that it was his right as the patriarch of our family to step in and dictate your future under Sharia Law, including the selection of your husband."

Mari grasped his hand. "And therefore, had the right to appoint Khalid as his representative in brokering the marriage."

Hope gasped. "But that's bullshit, right?" Her gaze darted between her parents. "I am officially an American citizen. They cannot impose Sharia Law on me."

Mari sighed. "Legally, no. But if Khalid kidnaps you and brings you back to Saudi Arabia, no one will stop him. They will protect *him*, not you. In Saudi Arabia, the men act as the legal guardians of female family members. No questions asked."

Harun nodded. "Even though my brother, Azar, technically controls the family now, he seems to have little control over Khalid. My brother agreed to the ban on arranged marriages when I handed over the reins, but when pushed, will he enforce it? I can't guarantee that, nor can I guarantee that he would intervene to keep you safe. I'm an outsider now. No longer a member of the family. I have no real influence."

Mari added, "And while the religion police no longer have the authority to arrest people for violations of Sharia Law, male family members have no reluctance in imposing it."

Cate's eyes narrowed. "Then why are we even involving Hope in this? It's too dangerous for her. Let me go in."

Cade shook his head. "Not only does Hope speak the language, but she also grew up in the Middle East. She understands the expectations and proper behavior for women in that society. She moves like she belongs. She responds to others as if she belongs. And more importantly, she knows what offends. That isn't something you can learn in a fortnight. It's ingrained from birth. That may be useful if we are detained."

Anders nodded. "Which is why we have to get in, snatch Alya, and get the hell out. However we use Hope, we need to keep her away from the authorities and anyone else who has put a target on her back."

"Hope, you can refuse the assignment if you think the risk is too great." Cade took a long sip of coffee. "You have more baggage than most, and that increases the danger to you. Say *no* and we will find another way."

Harun grunted. "Nice try. You know my daughter better than that."

Hope scowled at Cade. "I'm really hoping you asked only because you wanted to cover your ass with your buddy, my father. Because I never asked for preferential treatment and I don't want it now. I trust this team. We'll be working together. That's all I need."

Cade nodded, pleased. "Alright, then. Anders will be in charge on the ground. Hope, Tom, and Cate will make up his team. I'll be at the airport with your mother and father to supervise transport. We'll have Dianna on coms, at least initially. The WiFi setup there isn't very secure. We may have to resort to cell phones or go dark at some point. We have some work to do before we proceed, but I want wheels up in seventy-two hours. Let's get busy."

Anders swiped at the console, and a blueprint popped up on the whiteboard.

He turned to members of his team—Hope, Cate, and Tom. "This is where our target is being held. It's a small apartment building located on the outskirts of Fujairah City. Nahar's literary agent has spoken to her father and managed to get the exact location from him."

He highlighted a room on the blueprint. "She's being held in Apartment Two-Ten, on the first floor. And in case you're wondering, they have basement or garden apartments that have numbers beginning with one. You need to keep that in mind. She's on what we would consider the first floor. Our heat probe indicates that two bodies are in the apartment most of the time, though one often joins another outside the apartment in a hallway. There may be others outside the building, but we really won't know that until we get there."

Cate began to type something into her phone. She looked up. "Well, if they wanted to isolate her, they picked a good spot. Small population, one small airport with limited commercial flights, lots of coastline, only a few roadways in and out. If she managed to escape, Alya would be hard-pressed to find a way to safety. She would have to go via water, and that looks dicey at best. With all the tussles with Iran, the emirates have become especially vigilant about protecting their waterways."

She sighed. "This is going to be more than a snatch and grab. We are going to have to figure out how to get her out of the country quickly and safely. It's not like we can just head for the border. That area is on high alert, which means increased police—and possibly military—presence." She squinted at the phone. "The closest country is Oman, which is a good thing. They're friendly to the U.S. The other option is Saudi Arabia, which is clearly a no-go with Hope's potential problems with her brother. We may have to split up at the last minute."

Tom, also scrolling through his phone, added, "It looks like there are only two major roadways that lead to the border with Oman. The closest crossing point is about two hundred fifty miles by land, two hundred seventeen miles by water. So primary transport is the bus, hired car, or boat. That doesn't leave us with a lot of options."

Hope pulled out her phone and began searching. "Looks like the local airport only serves Abu Dhabi, but it does have a charter terminal. That may be the most efficient way out. What's the official status of our relationship with the UAE?"

"Supportive, but not necessarily friendly." Cade entered

the room with a bakery box and a supersized cup of coffee. "We assist them with border security and also assist in protecting their oil tankers from rogue nations, like Iran. Since the UAE was attacked earlier this year, they have really stepped up security on their coasts."

Hope frowned. "I thought Iran was cleared in those attacks."

Cade shook his head. "Not cleared. The investigators just couldn't find definitive proof. The U.S. Security Council claims the countries owning those tankers—the UAE, Norway, and Saudi Arabia—can't prove conclusively that Iran was involved, even though no one really doubts it. People are on edge. Things inside Iran are so unstable at the moment that those in charge may be seeking to trigger a military dispute elsewhere as a distraction."

Tom put his phone down. "So, if our relations are friendly, does that mean someone in the government on the up and up, someone not associated with her kidnapping, is likely to give us some assistance in getting Alya out of there?"

Cade chuckled. "Hope, why don't you answer that one?"

Hope smiled. "The UAE, like most of the countries in the Middle East, are governed by tribes or families. A friendly relationship only means that the government recognizes the U.S. as an ally. It doesn't mean the ruling family or any other families with influence will cooperate with the rescue of someone they see as their enemy—or a family member's enemy—on their home turf. Besides, we have no real legal standing and can make no official demands. Nahar isn't even a U.S. citizen or technically under our protection. They have no reason to cooperate with us.

"In fact, my research suggests they have a lot to lose. Remember, it is believed that Alya's book will reveal information on Middle Eastern countries that fund, shelter, or otherwise support terrorists. If that's the case, they can't afford to have that information fall into our hands. If we discover the government is working against us, our President *will* impose sanctions. Including the removal of military support."

Cade nodded. "We protect their waterways and ports. Primarily their oil exports. That's something they can't afford to lose."

Anders swiped at the console. "However, that doesn't mean we can't help ourselves. Sheikh Ali has contacts in and around the UAE who he believes will assist us. That's what he's working on now. For example, we can get a chartered jet into the Fujairah International Airport, it just can't be owned by Hope's family. And using a local charter company may raise suspicion. We need to borrow aircraft from someone we can trust. And then we need to find transport from the apartment building to the airport. That's where we need to get creative. How do we safely transport Alya out of the building without being seen?"

Tom tapped a pen on the table. Hope shot him an annoyed look and grabbed it out of his hand. "Stop it," she hissed.

The others laughed. Hope blushed.

Tom studied the blueprints on the whiteboard. "Does the apartment building have underground or off-street parking?"

Anders shook his head. "Neither. Remember, everything is built on sand. Nothing underground is particularly stable. And while parking is available on the streets, you don't see a lot of it simply because there's also not a lot of car ownership among the lower classes. The wealthier families all drive luxury automobiles, Bugattis, Ferraris, Rolls Royces, Bentleys, which they park in garages at their homes. Other people travel mainly by bus or cab."

Tom frowned. "That limits our choices, somewhat. We can't use an old Honda Civic and park it outside without creating suspicion. Maybe our best choice is to do it at night, unless we want to use the old movie trick and roll her up in a rug and throw her into the back of a van."

Anders pointed at him. "Hold that thought. We are trying to get a handle on typical traffic in and out of the building. We need to figure out a way to enter and exit without raising flags."

Cate leaned forward. "Do you have any rooftop photos? Could we land a helicopter on the roof and whisk Alya off to the airport that way? We could be gone before anyone raised an alarm."

"We already checked that out. There is no way the roof would support the weight."

Cate persisted, "Then what about a ladder or lift? Maybe if we can get her to the roof, they could simply —"

Anders shook his head, again. "By all accounts, it's a quiet neighborhood. There is no way we can mask the sound of a helicopter. It will focus too much attention on us. People might think they are under attack and start shooting." He gazed at his team. "So other than the rug removal, any other ideas?"

Hope nodded. "We do it in plain sight. Cate and I will be wearing an abaya and hajib. An abaya is just a headcover, but a hajib has a face scarf as well. While Western dress is not unheard of, it is frowned upon and would make us stand out. Traditional dress permits us to move about without suspicion."

Cade opened the donut box and pulled out a cruller. He took a bite and waved the donut at her. "Unless that area has a curfew for women. Something else we need to find out."

Anders reached over and pulled a Bavarian crème donut from the box. He studied it, then took a bite. He smirked when some custard dripped down his chin. Cate handed him a napkin. After he cleaned up, he said, "So we need to verify a couple of things. Normal traffic in and out of the building, the existence of a curfew for women, the extent of security on

Alya, building security, and security on the area streets. We need to know who is watching and when." He pointed at Cade. "We also need to know if the Brits or any other allies have Alya in their sights. They could really fuck us over."

Cade popped the last piece of his donut in his mouth and wiped his hands on a napkin. "The Brits most definitely are watching. We confirmed their interest today. Not sure about any other allies, though. That's why you need to move quickly and play dirty. Let no one else interfere." He scowled. "And Cate, if you spot Tillie anywhere in the area, take her out. Don't ask and we won't tell. She almost got Dianna killed in South America. As far as I'm concerned, MISix still owes us for that one, and I will not play nice."

Cate nodded. She said sweetly, "I would be happy to take that bitch to the ground. I still say she was in with the cult, not acting on behalf of MISix. Nothing she did was in anyone's interests but her own."

Anders grinned. "And I am with you one hundred percent. I just may force-feed her some Foxglove. Poison her like she tried to do to Dianna. I almost lost my wife, and she got nothing more than a slap on the wrist. I want a piece of her, too."

Cade cleared his throat. "You can get your revenge on your own time. Right now, our only concern has to be getting Nahar out of that hidey-hole in the UAE. However, if Brit Barbie does make an appearance and attempts to interfere, you are within your rights to put her out of commission." He flashed an evil smile. "Temporarily, of course."

CHAPTER EIGHT: THE CHASE

Hope peered around the corner of the building.
"I spot three watchers," she said softly into the communications device in her ear. "One sitting in the café across the street, pretending he's reading a newspaper, wearing an ugly suit with bad shoes, and the other hanging in the doorway with another doofus, sucking on a cigarette." She turned and walked back to Anders, who was positioned at the back of the alley between buildings. "How do you want to handle this, boss? Going in the front door is not an option."

Anders spoke into his com. "Tom? Any luck in jimmying that back door?"

"Almost got it. It's an electronic lock. Dianna is walking me through dismantling it. Almost . . . there." Tom grunted. "Got it. Pretty nice having a digital locksmith on call twenty-four-seven. Even remotely. That worked like a charm. The alarm didn't even sound."

"Good to know," Anders replied.

"But be prepared for a silent one, too," Dianna's voice came over the com. "They just may have a backup if they consider Alya a high-risk captive. Look for trip plates and wires on your way in. Do a sweep with your night vision goggles when you get inside. That should pick up the heat sensors. I may have to shut down the power."

"That's why you told us to bring the goggles, even though it's still daytime," Tom replied. "I thought you were overdoing it a bit."

Dianna growled into the com.

Anders sighed. It was comforting to have his wife with them, even if she was sitting in a control room near D.C. When Dianna has stepped down from field duty instead of assuming a role in the training division and as Janet's replacement as the chief locksmith, safecracker, and computer hacker, Anders had been relieved. A married couple working together on dangerous missions was complicated, and when Dianna had almost died in South America, Anders had learned how easy it was to lose his shit. His focus had been on finding his wife, rather than their overall objective.

Cade had managed to pull him back in before he totally blew it. Now, while Anders was sure Dianna missed the field, having her safe and out of harm's way allowed him to fully focus on his job, which right now, was getting Alya Nahar safely to the United States.

"Cate?" Anders asked. "Any stalkers behind the building? In nearby alleyways? Is the back door the better option?"

"Surprisingly, the alleys are clear and no snipers appear to be set up on any nearby rooftops," she responded. "There is a camera over the door, which Dianna has already bypassed. If there are no silent alarms inside, we are in the clear. We should be good to go."

"And if there are tripwires and sensor plates, Hope may be the only option to get inside," Dianna said. "The tripwires would be set high on the wall and the sensor plates would require one hundred pounds of weight before they are triggered. Otherwise, every cat, dog, child, or other critters would set them off. Hope's just under a hundred pounds, and at five feet, is unlikely to trip any wires or sensors."

"Tom, open the door and make a sweep," Anders ordered. "Let's see what we're walking into."

The sound of a door opening could be heard. "There it is," Dianna said softly. "There's a tripwire right inside the door, and one compression tile further in. I'm guessing there are more. Tom, sneak under the wire and get a shot down the hallway." There was silence.

"Okay," Dianna said. "Two more plates, set in the center of the floor. All you have to do is stick to the walls when moving in. I don't see any more wires, but stay alert anyway. I don't want to have to shut down the power. If they have electronic locks on the door to Alya's apartment and I cut the power, you will have to blow the door, and that will alert the guys out front."

"Okay, let's make this quick and clean, guys," Anders said. He turned to Hope. "Enter the back way and do your thing. Distract them and make them follow you. Dianna will track you on GPS and the com, but communicate only if necessary. We don't know who's listening. Run like hell and do not stop for any reason. Get to the pre-arranged pickup point and to the airport. Understood?"

Hope nodded.

"Once we leave the building, the rest of us go silent. Our coms will be turned off. Too many signals from one area will provide a beacon for anyone who's looking. You all have your Bat Signals. If we get separated and you need help, use them."

"Got it," Hope said with a nod. "And for the record, wearing protective armor under this robe really sucks. I'm sweating like a pig in heat. Damn hot."

Cate smirked. "She's right. And I'm not even wearing a Ninja suit. I'm sweating so much that I'm almost slippery."

"Hey, my robes are no picnic either," Tom replied. "And mine stink," he muttered. "I think they picked this off some guy who spent a month in the desert without taking a shower. Almost smells like a camel."

"Pipe down, guys," Anders snapped. "Hope? Ready?"

"Roger."

Ander said, "It's a go, folks. Green light. Let's bring Alya home."

Hope entered the back door and ducked under the trip-wire, avoiding the first sensor plate. She silently moved down the empty hallway until she reached another. She peered around the corner, then pulled back. "Two guards, both armed, but they're sitting on the floor, playing cards. Easy pickings. I could just take them out."

"Follow the plan, Hope," Anders snarled. "Get them out the front door and away from the building. I want them and everyone else in pursuit. We'll let you know when we're clear."

"Got it."

Hope rounded the corner and crept up to the guards. "Boo!" she hissed in Arabic. The men stared at her, surprised and dropped their cards. She then dropped the scarf covering her mouth and nose, revealing her heavily made-up face and grinned at the men.

One of them said, "How did you get out of your room?"

Hope laughed. "I'll never tell." She started to move away. "Maybe you should have locked the bathroom window," she taunted.

The man reached for her, but Hope kicked his arm. "Catch me if you can, you old goats," she yelled in Arabic then began to run. She burst through the front door, knocking aside the two men on the steps, and ran into the street. She heard the other men come through the door, yelling and arguing, but all of them followed. Hope ran up the street and turned the corner. She darted quickly into a street market, dodging around shoppers and stalls. She let the man in the lead get close, then she sprinted away. It was a game of cat and mouse, but this time, she wasn't the prey.

Damn. They are moving way too slowly. I need to keep them on my tail. Hope ducked behind a stall and crawled under a table. She waited until she saw the feet of her pursuers approach. She jumped up on the table and began to yell, "Help me! I am

Alya Nahar. One of the disappeared. Your leaders kidnapped me and have been holding me captive. Help me. Please help me."

The people shopping at the stalls began to murmur and move forward with interest, but four of the guards pulled out guns and aimed them at the crowd. Most shrugged, shook their heads, and turned away. The fifth man, in the ill-fitting suit, aimed his gun directly at Hope. Knowing full well her Ninja suit repelled bullets, Hope giggled and did a little dance.

"Come here, little girl," he shouted, his voice harsh. "You have nowhere to go. If you don't surrender and end this spectacle, I will shoot you." He clicked off the safety from his gun. "And then I will shoot everyone in this market, maybe even your family."

"Hope? What the fuck is going on?" Dianna's voice was filled with concern. "You stopped moving." She paused. "Dammit, Hope. Stick to the plan. Get a move on."

"Gotcha," Hope said. She jumped off the table, yelled an obscenity in Arabic, and ran out of the market, down a dusty road. The map of the small city played out in her head. Left, two rights, then straight ahead. Hope heard a shot ring out and increased her speed. She ducked into an alley and ripped off her gown, leaving only her black body suit. She pulled up the hood and continued to run down the alley. When she reached another road, she turned right. Hope heard more shots, but her pursuers were now a block away.

As she rounded another corner, a man jumped in front of her, a gun aimed at her head. "Those guards may be stupid men," he spat in heavily accented English, "but I am not."

"Hope, dammit, keep moving!" Dianna yelled into the com.

"Got a problem, here," Hope muttered. She stared at the man, stunned. *Where the hell did he come from?* Hope backed up against the building, pretending to be afraid. She could hear her other pursuers approaching. The man drew closer and reached for her, his gun still aimed at her head. "No, no, no," she mumbled in Arabic.

"Hope? Do you need help? Dammit, use the Bat Signal if you need help!" Dianna's voice was frantic.

A malevolent grin crossed the man's face. "We are everywhere, little girl. There was never any real possibility of an escape."

Hope sprang from the wall and batted the man's gun from his hand. She kicked him in the balls, and when he collapsed with a groan, she kicked him in the head. He collapsed onto the ground. She heard shouts, much closer now, and she again began to run.

"All clear," she shouted.

When she reached the next corner, another small crowd was gathered. Men dressed in native dress, thawbs and keffiyeh, were milling around, clearly waiting for something. Hope skidded to a halt. *Damn it. They're standing in the way of my ride.*

Anders waited for Hope to lead the guards away from the building. "Okay, she's got the attention of all of the tails. There goes one, two, three, four, five."

Cate laughed into the com. "She'll lead all of them on a merry dance."

Anders moved out onto the road. "Tom? Are the hallways clear?"

"Looks like it."

"Okay, be prepared for one more inside the apartment. You're on the guard. Cate, grab Nahar. I'll have the car waiting."

Anders heard a door open and a woman screamed. There was a scuffle. Then a crash.

"Sorry about that," Cate said. "Alya grabbed a lamp and swung it at us. We didn't get a chance to give her an I.D. Figured it was safer to subdue than explain."

"Any *unfriendlies*?"

"Nope. Guess the inside guy was playing cards. They didn't even have her tied up. Cocky bastards." Cate paused. "I've got her purse. There's no passport. Only an I.D." Cate could be heard in the background, speaking soothingly. "It's okay, Ms. Nahar. We're friends. We're going to get you out of here and to the U.S. You'll be safe there." The woman began to wail. "Dammit," Cate said. "I'm going to have to . . ." There was silence. "Sorry, dear, we don't have time for histrionics."

Anders groaned. "Did you really have to knock her out?"

Cate laughed. "It was either that or gag her. I just tapped her carotid sinus, activated the baroreceptor. She'll be out for a few minutes, enough time to get her transferred."

"God, Cate, you should have been a doctor."

Cate snickered. "Or a kidnapper. I know all of the pressure points. When my bodyguards got bored, they taught me how to knock out overenthusiastic suitors. It's been a useful skill."

"I'll bet." Anders approached a late model BMW, unlocked it, and slipped inside. "She doesn't need a passport. We're headed straight to the charter terminal and onto the U.N.'s plane. No one will check." Anders pushed the ignition button and moved the car up in front of the building. "I'm outside. Cate, resecure the door as you leave, then hold the rest of them open for Tom. I assume he needs to carry Nahar out of there. Let's get a move on, people, before someone gets suspicious."

"Any word from Hope?" Tom asked.

"Negative," Anders replied. "As far as I know, she's still on the move. Dianna is monitoring her. No reason to worry."

Cate threw open the back door of the car, and Tom slid past her with Alya's limp body. Then she slammed the door and hopped into the passenger seat.

"Okay, let's roll." Anders put the car in drive and pulled out into the road. No one appeared to be watching. In fact, the street was pretty much empty. Only a few cars passed them.

Cate removed her abaya, revealing a generic flight attendant's uniform. She popped a hat on her head, then blew out a breath. "Damn, I wish I was wearing a bikini under this. Crank up the A/C, would you? I feel like a wet noodle." She scrunched her nose. "I hope no one notices these wrinkles on my uniform." She gazed at Tom. "Lose the thawb and the headpiece, then I'll switch places with you. I need to get Alya out of that getup."

Tom pulled off his robe and his headscarf, revealing a pilot's uniform. He pulled out a hat and placed it on his head.

Cate grinned. "Man, you look hot. I'd fly you!"

Tom snorted. "Over Hope's dead body."

Cate snickered. "She ain't wearing a ring, so until you bring that bling . . ."

Anders groaned. "Cate, focus."

Cate gestured to Tom to move out of the way. She lowered the back of her seat and crawled over. Tom moved to the front, then pushed the seat back up.

"We have a tail," Anders muttered. "Embassy plates."

Cate turned and studied the car. "Nice Bentley. Definitely an Embassy car. One woman, one man. The woman is white as the driven snow. Blonde. Could be Tillie. Guy is in native dress. Never seen him before," She pulled out her phone and took a photo. "For future reference." In an exaggerated British accent, Cate said, "I dare say, Holmes, we have ourselves two birdwatchers. We must take flight."

Anders pressed down on the accelerator, leaving the car a distance behind. "As you wish, my dear," he replied with his own bad British accent. "It is time to outfox the hounds."

Tom laughed. "Not sure how much horsepower that car

has, but Bentleys are a bit cumbersome. They bottom out easily. Some off-roading might be wise."

"Gotcha," Anders said. He gazed into the rearview mirror. "How is Nahar doing?"

Cate tugged at Nahar. "I hope she wakes up soon. This is going to be like dressing a tree stump." She shook the woman and Nahar moaned. "Oh, thank God. She's waking up."

Nahar's large brown eyes slowly opened. Her gaze landed on Cate and startled, she sat up. Her focus darted to the men in the front seat. She opened her mouth as if preparing to scream.

Cate clapped a hand over her mouth. "It's alright, Alya," Cate said quickly in Arabic, then English. "You fainted, and we couldn't wait to revive you because we had to move quickly. We need to get you changed and out of your abaya. Okay?"

Alya nodded, and Cate removed her hand. A confused expression crossed Alya's face. "Americans?" she said with an elegant British accent. A soft sob escaped her. "Oh, thank Allah." A look of panic entered her eyes. "Wait. We can't go. Stop. We must go back."

Cate frowned. "Why?"

"My parents are still here. They will toss them in prison or worse. We must get them!"

Cate squeezed her hands. "They're already on the plane, waiting for you. We scooped them up yesterday."

Alya pulled off her abaya and hijab, revealing a light cotton slip. She quickly pulled on the flight attendant uniform, a blouse and skirt, then thumped Anders on the shoulder. "Step on it."

"Check her for trackers," Anders said. "I don't like the fact that we picked up a tail so easily. Everyone should be chasing Hope. Dump anything they've given her to wear. Pitch it out the window."

Cate gestured at Alya. "What do you have on that didn't belong to you before they grabbed you?"

"The abaya. The hijab. And the sandals. They took my shoes and gave me these sandals."

"Bet it's the shoes," Tom said. "Better toss everything." He flushed. "I hate to ask, but are your underthings new or did they give those to you, too?"

Alya stared at him. Slowly, she said, "They gave them to me, but I wash them daily, so there is no way they could have attached a bug."

Tom nodded. "Just the outer clothing and the sandals, then."

Alya handed them to Cate. She opened the window and threw them onto the road. "Anything else?" Cate asked. "Jewelry? A watch? A hair tie?"

Alya shook her head. "They took anything personal. They wanted to make me feel truly alone. I was to have nothing that brought me comfort."

Cate smiled. "Okay, then. Finish getting dressed. We are a flight crew trying to catch our plane. We need to look the part." She peered at Alya's face. "We need to remove your makeup, too. Less is more in this case. We want you to look like a different person."

Alya nodded. She took the wet cleansing cloth Cate handed her and began wiping her face. "Where are we headed?" she asked.

"If all goes well, the airport, Heathrow, then the United States," Anders said. "We can protect you best there." He took a hard right, then a left into a small alley that led to a one-way street. "Glad I checked this out last night. No way a Bentley can get through here, and if they try to whip around the block, they'll be facing into traffic. Hopefully, by the time they get clear, we'll be long gone."

Anders pulled out onto the street, tires squealing, and sped toward the airport.

Cate looked out the back window. The Bentley was stopped at the entrance to the alley. Hopefully, they had lost their tail. For now.

Anders raced into the Fujairah International Airport, bypassed the main passenger terminal, and drove around to the Executive Business Jet Terminal. Numerous private jets were parked on the tarmac or in hangers. Sitting at the end of the single runway was an unmarked Gulfstream 650. As the car approached the plane, a ramp lowered on the back end and Anders drove into the cargo bay. He waited for two workers to anchor the car and close the cargo door.

Tom turned and smiled at Alya. "You'll be leaving in a few minutes. Let's get you upstairs."

Alya frowned. "You aren't coming with me?"

Anders shook his head. "Sorry, but our assignment ends here. We're turning you over to Lydia Creighton and her staff. She's the U.S. Ambassador to the U.N. You'll be in the air before anyone even knows you're missing. At least no one will try to tail you and shoot you down. No one messes with Ambassador Creighton."

Cate tried not to smile at the description of her mother. "Your safety is our primary concern," she added. "Believe me, you are much safer with the U.N. than us."

Alya appeared uncomfortable and tears filled her eyes. "It's just that . . ."

Cate gazed at her. "I know. You want to stay with your rescuers. But your family is upstairs. And all of you are now safe. The Ambassador will get you to the U.S., maybe help you get your book published, and then get you resettled wherever you choose to live."

"I want to stay in the U.S.," Alya said firmly. "The British promised to protect me, but they failed. I no longer trust them.

They just wanted my book before it was published. I'm sure they felt they had a right to censor it." She sniffed and her eyes narrowed. "They do not have clean hands in this." She snorted. "The British have a history of bad judgment. That's why they almost lost WWII. They tried to play nice with Hitler." She shook her head. "What fools. You Americans had to save their hides then, and you may have to now."

The group left the car and headed up to the passenger lounge, where Cade, Ambassador Creighton, and Alya's parents waited. She immediately went into her mother's arms.

Cade acknowledged their arrival with a nod. "Any problems?" he asked Anders.

Anders rolled his eyes. "Other than the Brits trying to butt in, things went fine, really. The locals fell for the bait—hook, line, and sinker. Hope should be right behind us."

Cade stood and nodded at the Ambassador. "Thanks for your help. We'll see you in the U.S." He gestured at the rest of the team. "Come on, we have a plane to catch."

Anders cast off his thawb and headdress, revealing a pilot's uniform. He pulled a hat on his head. He smiled at Alya. "Safe travels, my friend."

Another man in a utilitarian blue suit opened the door and lowered the stairway. "Quickly, now. Your jet is right behind us."

The four agents hustled down the steps. When Cate reached the tarmac, the stairs retracted and the door slammed shut. The engines on the plane fired and it began to roll away. Cate clapped her hands over her ears. "Jesus, that's loud."

Cade grabbed her hand. "Come on, we have a plane to catch."

CHAPTER NINE: CONSEQUENCES

Hope swallowed and her stride faltered. Suddenly fear punched her in the gut and all decisiveness left her. *Dammit! I can't get caught in this country. People are after my father and will use me as leverage to get to him. And others are after me. Rami. My brother. God knows who else. If they catch me, I'm as good as dead. Dammit. I should have stuck to the plan. I should not have stopped in the market. Stupid. Stupid. Stupid.* Her eyes narrowed as she considered the angry mob in front of her. *Do I try to run through them or do I run the other way?*

"Hope! Talk to me!" Dianna shouted into the com. "Do you need help?"

Hope could hear a car approaching behind her. The crowd in front of her was moving closer. *What the fuck am I supposed to do?* "I'm going to try to run the gauntlet," Hope muttered.

"What? Hope, no! Run around them. It's too dangerous. Run the other way, you'll be picked . . ."

Hope ignored Dianna. She took a deep breath and ran directly into the crowd. She was fast and small and wearing a slippery ninja suit. Surely, she could get past them to the transportation that awaited her.

Hope ran hard into the crowd of angry old men. She managed to take them by surprise. She broke through the line and was almost free of them. Then someone grabbed her by the hood of her ninja suit and spun her around. Someone else tripped her. She started to fall and attempted to roll away, but someone grabbed her hair and held firmly. *Damn.* Hope kicked and scratched. She tried every defensive tactic she could, but now more hands were grabbing at her and taking hold. Someone snatched an arm, another a leg. She couldn't break free.

Desperately, she said into her com, "I'm in trouble. I need backup. *Now.* Mayday. Mayday. *Help!*"

Still struggling against her captors, Hope was carried off the road into an alley. Panic rose within her. *This is not good.* She was thrown on the ground, and the men surrounded her, trapping her against the wall of a building. She had nowhere to run. She looked up into a sea of malevolent eyes. With a sinking heart, she knew without a doubt that these men intended serious harm. Finally, Hope did the one thing she swore she would never do. She bit down on the device implanted in the back of her mouth and activated the Bat Signal. *Please God, let them get to me in time before this crowd kills me.*

They kicked at her. Some pummeled her with their arms. Other threw rocks at her. One man beat her with his cane. They shouted insults in Arabic. *Whore! Devil! Infidel! Traitor! Sinner! Bitch! Slut!*

Hope was confused. These men were not the police. Why had they descended on her? Her eyes searched the crowd and her gaze met a pair of eyes so similar to her own. *Khalid. Her brother.* In Arabic, Hope shouted, "Khalid! Why are you doing this?"

"Because you consort with the Infidels," he shouted back in English. He spat on her. "My father has turned you into an American whore. We will beat Satan out of you. You must pay. *That* is our law."

The beating continued, and Hope felt her strength, her will to live, begin to slip away. She had never felt such pain. Tears poured from her eyes as she curled tightly into a ball and turned toward the wall, no longer fighting to ward off the blows. She heard Dianna's voice in her head. "Protect your head, Hope. Above else, protect your head. We're coming. Someone is coming." Instinct took over and Hope tucked her head between her arms. *Please. Someone help me.* Hope could not stop the sobs that wracked her body.

A shot rang out. Was it was aimed at her? She was in so much pain, a bullet to the head would be a welcome relief. She tried to make herself smaller. Another bullet rang out. Then another. She heard shouts and an argument, but Hope had retreated so far into her head, she could no longer translate the words. The crowd fell silent and Hope sensed that people were moving away. The problem was, her body was frozen. She couldn't run. Hell, she couldn't even move.

"Hope! Talk to me! Please, talk to me!" Dianna's plea seemed otherworldly as if she was speaking from the great beyond.

Hope felt arms close around her and she whimpered. *They've got me now. They are going to kill me. I'm sorry. I'm so damn sorry.* The blackness was beckoning.

She heard a voice murmuring to her and she fought to understand. As her eyes pulled closed, she heard a voice, a familiar one. "I've got you, pipsqueak. I've got you."

Hope moaned, then everything went black.

Warren Hazelton carried Hope's limp body to a dusty old BMW, a car his boss, Sheikh Ali, had procured from a friend. He and his fellow bodyguard, Andrew Sullivan—Sully to his colleagues and friends—had been assigned to pick up Hope and transport her to the airport. When she had been late, they began looking for her. Then Cade had notified them that she was in trouble.

Thank God they had spotted the angry mob.

He gently placed Hope on the back seat. "Jesus, they kicked the shit of her. She's got internal injuries for sure, not sure about broken bones, but probably some ribs. In this Ninja suit, it's too difficult to tell. Too bad the damn suit only protects her from bullets, not sticks and stones." He pressed his fingers against her neck. "She's got a pulse, but it's fluttery. Damn it, she's so tiny. She isn't built to withstand a beating like that. She's going to need a doctor."

Sully turned and studied her bloodied body. "This is my worst nightmare. When we were protecting her as a kid, we at least had some control over who she interacted with. There was no way we could have predicted this." He pushed a button on his phone and said, "We've got her, boss. But she's hurt, bad. I don't think we can risk taking her by road to Oman. She needs medical help, and fast!"

"Bloody hell, get her to the plane," her father replied over the speakerphone. "We've got medical supplies. We're just going to have to wing it." He paused. "Can I speak to her?"

"No can do, sir." Sully downshifted and pulled back into the street. "She's barely conscious."

"*Please.*"

"You can try, sir," Sully said. "Not sure she can hear you." He handed the phone to Hazelton. "Hold it to her ear."

Hazelton gently set the phone down next to Hope's head. "Go ahead, sir."

There was silence, then in a soft tenor, Harun began to sing in Arabic. A lullaby.

Hope shifted and a slight smile crossed her face. Then she moaned. "Daddy," she whispered.

Harun continued to sing.

"She's smiling, sir. She hears you."

Harun stopped. "Good. We will need to move quickly when you get here. Nahar is gone, but that doesn't mean the authorities won't still come after *us.*"

"Understood, sir," Sully replied. "We're about five minutes out. We'll need help with transfer."

"Put the phone back to her ear. I'll continue to sing to her until you get here."

Hazelton set the phone between the seat and Hope's ear.

Harun could be heard singing softly.

"Get her ready, how?" Hazelton asked Sully, keeping his voice low. "I'm afraid to move her. We need a gurney. We have to stabilize her body somehow. If we move her, we may do more harm than good. I probably shouldn't have moved her at all, but I had to get her away from that mob."

"Improvise."

Hazelton looked around the car, then searched the floor. "The best I've got is one of those dual floor mats. It's pretty small, but it's fairly thick."

"Hope's light and she's tiny. It will have to work, man." The car entered the airport. "One minute to transfer. *Be ready.*"

The car's tires squealed as he hit the gas.

In the background, Harun's voice could still be heard, singing softly. Crooning another lullaby.

Cade could hear Harun's words clearly as he stood just outside the door to the cockpit.

"It's all right, sweetheart. You're almost here. We've got you. You're going to be fine." He choked up. "We love you. Always." He paused, and Cade knew he was fighting to keep his voice calm, reassuring. "I'm going to go now. Get everything ready so we can get you on the plane. Hang in there. I'll see you soon." He disconnected his phone.

"We've got her, Dianna," Cade muttered into his phone. "I'm signing off. I'll get back to you." *Damn. Of all the people to get hurt. This was going to hit everyone hard. Especially Harun and Mari.* Quickly, he sent a text to Janet. Someone was going to have to start making arrangements, no matter what the outcome. Janet could do it best from the U.S.

"Cade!" Harun called from the cockpit. "We've got incoming and they need help!"

Cade straightened his shoulders and stepped into the

cockpit. Harun's head was buried in his hands. "I know, old man," he said. "We've got this." He squeezed his shoulder. "Get prepared for take-off. We have a medical school dropout on board. Nurse-trained. Better than a medic. But the sooner we get Hope to a medical facility, the better. Call Ramstein Air Base in Germany. That's our best bet."

Cade left the cockpit and snapped, "Listen up, people. We've got Hope, but she's hurt. Cate, get your kit. You're going to be playing doctor." He attempted to inject some levity. "As in scalpels and sutures. Not the kinky kind."

Cate shook her head and muttered, "Really?" She stood and began exploring the overhead bins. She pulled out a large duffle. "Got it. We need a place to set up. I need to lay her flat to do an examination." She gazed at Mari, who was pale, her expression anxious. "There's a bedroom in back, correct? Can I use that?"

Mari nodded. "Of course." She stood. "Follow me. I'll help you set up." Mari gazed at Cate. "Your mother will be pleased that all that medical training you never used finally came in handy."

Cate smirked. "After the first year, I was so bored, I thought I was going to lose it. Law school worked out much better." They disappeared into the back of the plane.

Cade opened the plane's door and lowered the stairs. "Anders and Tom, get down there and help with the transfer. We have no idea what condition she's in."

"Crap," Tom said. "I knew this was a bad idea."

Cade slapped him on the back. "Buck up, man. She needs us. Now is not the time to wuss out."

Tom glared at him but nodded.

Anders punched Tom on the arm. "Told you the first time is hard. Come on, we owe it to Hope to get the job done. She risked her life for Nahar."

They headed down the stairs while Cade waited on the

plane. He watched as a dusty black BMW pulled up to the steps. Hazelton jumped out and began issuing instructions. Anders bent down and grabbed one end of the floor mat. Tom ran around the back of the car, opened the back door, and grabbed the other end.

Sully turned off the car and joined him.

Cade watched as they rolled Hope onto the mat, then set it back down on the seat and began to slide it out from the car. Hazelton held one end, Anders grabbed the middle, and Tom caught the other end.

"God, she's light as a feather," Anders said. He studied her bruised body. "They really worked her over." He nodded at Hazelton. "Good thing you were close. They might have killed her."

"Looks like they tried. They were throwing rocks at her when we got there," Hazelton said. "We were two blocks away, waiting for her. When she didn't show, we went looking. Thank God for that Bat Signal." He gazed at Anders. "Someone got that mob wound up. That was one angry crowd. We got lucky." His face faltered and his eyes watered. "*Real* lucky."

They pulled Hope's body from the car and began to carry her up the stairs. Her hair and face were matted with blood. Bruises were already forming around her right eye. One arm hung limply off the faux stretcher.

Cade watched Tom carefully, When Agents got involved with one another, things always got tricky. It was tough enough to see a fellow agent get hurt. But when it was a fellow agent you loved, well, then things just got dicey. And Cade had no doubt Tom loved Hope. Harun had told him the guy was already ring shopping.

His wife, Janet, had dropped out of the Agency for this very reason. Working with his lover was bad enough. Working with his wife and the mother of his children was just plain dangerous. It was too hard to focus when the woman you loved was at risk. Even Anders had learned that the hard way. When Dianna almost died at the God's Delight compound in Peru, he had been terrified and was about to act irrationally, putting them both in even more danger. Ultimately, the couple had decided the risk was too great. Dianna had transferred into training and taken over Janet's role as the master hacker, safecracker, and locksmith. He suspected the discussion he'd had with them was about to be repeated with Tom and Hope.

Some couples were able to compartmentalize in the field, setting emotion aside. Cade was sure Hope was one of them. However, he suspected Tom was not.

As they moved past him with the stretcher, Cade said softly, "Now's not the time to lose it, Tom. Hope needs you. She needs *us* to be strong. Your distress will cause *her* distress. If I have to, I will keep you away from her."

"Yes, sir," Tom responded. His voice was halting. "I just didn't get it. And I certainly didn't expect this. My God, we all thought Hope was Wonder Woman. We screwed up. We let her down. No way should we have let her run wild on her own."

Cade gazed at Anders as they reached the top step of the ramp. "That's for another day, Tom. Right now, we need to focus — on saving Hope."

Cate walked out of the bedroom and stripped off her bloodied gloves. She pulled a plastic bag out of her pocket and dropped them inside. "I'll need a garbage bag for medical waste," she said to Anders. "Standard procedure." She gazed at Cade. "How far are we from Ramstein Air Force Base?"

"We're about four hours out, though I'm sure Harun is pushing this plane as fast as it will go."

Cate nodded. "Good. The sooner the better. Chances are she wouldn't have made it to Heathrow, much less Dulles. She has a lot of bruising in her pelvic area and more on her back. She's lost a fair amount of blood. And her blood pressure is pretty low. We almost lost her once when it bottomed out. I had to use the portable defibrillator. I suspect there is some internal bleeding, but she doesn't seem to be in a lot of distress. Still, she took some hits. The Ninja suit didn't protect her much. She's so tiny, with very little body fat. She had no real padding to protect her from their blows. Maybe that's something we need to consider in the future."

Cade nodded but said nothing.

Cate fell down into a seat and sighed. "Mari cleaned up the cuts, I did the stitching. At least we could do something."

"Is she awake?" Tom asked.

Cate shook her head. "She was in a lot of pain, so I sedated her. She obviously protected her head from the assault, so there appears to be little damage there. She'll have a black eye, though. Someone must have gotten a punch in. As far as I can tell, she has a broken wrist and a sprained ankle. All I had were splints, but I stabilized the wrist the best I could and iced the ankle. The best thing we can do is keep her still. And *pray*." Cate stood. "Mari's with her. I need to talk to Harun." She walked to the cockpit.

"She was barely conscious by the time I got to her," Hazelton said. "She might not remember what happened."

Anders scowled. "Who was that mob, anyway? Where did they even come from? And how did they know where to find her? It certainly wasn't Nahar's guards, that's for sure. They would have just used their guns. It had to be someone else. That mob was organized and probably waiting. Do we have a leak?"

Tom cocked an eyebrow. "Maybe it was random. Wrong place at the wrong time? A response to a woman wearing nothing but a Ninja suit? I mean, those things are pretty re-vealing."

Hazelton shook his head. "They had her in an alley right off the road leading to the pickup point. They knew she was coming that way." He gazed at Cade. "You might have had more eyes on her than you thought. There is no way those guards called ahead and set this up. Someone knew her path in advance, which means audio surveillance. Someone was listening in at the planning stages. Tracking her somehow. It's an easy bug, on phones, on a person, in the room. It could even be on this plane, even though this is registered to some-one else.

"Someone talked and someone with an ax to grind heard them. This was personal. I guarantee it. Someone saw an op-portunity and took advantage of it." He scowled. "The Agency fucked up, big guy."

Cade flushed, but again said nothing.

Tom frowned. "But how? We were in and out in less than twenty-four hours. No one even knew we were there."

"It was Khalid. Harun's son. The one who's so obsessed with Sharia Law. The one who still has a price on my hus-band's head." Mari stood in the doorway to the bedroom. "She keeps murmuring his name. He had to have been in-volved. I think she saw him."

Tom frowned "But how? We were so careful."

"He has watchers all over the Middle East, probably at every airport," Mari said. "Someone must have seen some-thing and tipped him off. I am guessing someone associated with the planes Harun borrowed or the cars that were pro-vided. That's a different world there. Loyalty is a slippery slope. People have a price. They can be bought or threatened or blackmailed. It could have been as simple as Harun's cousin mentioning he had to drop off cars for an American relative. The right ears would have perked up and passed it on to someone willing to pay. Khalid has made no secret of his animosity toward his father. He would have paid, and well."

Mari paused and sighed. Her eyes were red and weary. "He could have killed her, you know. She may be his sister, but she is also a mere woman who consorts with Infidels. A poor substitute for his real target, his father. But a substitute nonetheless." A sad expression crossed her face. "What kind of madness justifies doing this to your own sister? My God."

Mari tried to smile at Hazelton, then Sully. "I wasn't happy when Harun injected you into this mission, but I am so glad he did." A single tear dripped from her eye. "He understood the danger and kept you two close. You saved her life." She grabbed Hazelton's hand. "I can't thank you enough."

She gazed at Cade. "I suspect this throws a whole new light on how you use Hope from now on. Obviously, she can't be effective when she has people gunning for her personally as well as professionally. But don't you dare consider taking her out of the game. That *would* kill her." She rubbed her forehead. "Somehow, she'll heal. She won't give up."

Chapter Ten: We Did Not Interfere Enough

The tall stout man sat in his maroon leather office chair and sighed. It creaked as he rocked back and forth, examining the document in front of him. Absently, he ran his hand through his thick white hair, disrupting a formerly perfectly coifed head. Then he glared at the two people who sat before him.

"Agent Spencer, the Americans have requested an interview—in person. They claim you have interfered in two of their recent missions, endangering, indeed almost killing their agents." He scowled. "Care to explain?"

Tillie knew this was coming. She tugged at a lock of her hair, her eyes wide. "I have no idea why they would request such a thing." She gazed at Abdul Ali, then said firmly, "We did nothing that was not in pursuit of our objective." She nonchalantly cocked an eyebrow. "The fact that we failed speaks to our caution. In fact, we did not interfere enough."

Abdul nodded in agreement.

Tillie frowned. "Wait, how did they even know I was there?"

"One of their agents took a photo with their cell phone. They are not unfamiliar with you. You were easily identified." He tugged at his ear and sighed. "That may be a problem in the future. Fortunately, they were not as successful in identifying Abdul."

Abdul smiled. "Must have been the headdress. To the

Americans, I imagine men in keffiyeh all look alike."

The man snorted. "Well, blondes like Tillie do stick out in that area of the world." He studied them. "Humor me. Take me through your activities in the UAE, step-by-step."

Tillie took a deep breath. "Well, sir, upon your instructions, we proceeded to the UAE and checked in at the British Embassy in Dubai. Wireless intercepts from our operatives there led us to believe that our target was being held in Fujairah. So we proceeded to that city to investigate."

"And what did you find?"

"Although we were able to find the suspected site, we were unable to verify the presence of Alya Nahar on the premises, sir."

"So?"

"We decided to remain in the city, surveil the building for twenty-four-hours to assess any unusual activity, sir," Abdul said.

"And?"

"Our assessment was inconclusive, sir," Tillie said. "So, because Abdul is of Middle Eastern descent and was wearing traditional dress, we thought he could approach the building without raising suspicion. We determined that it would be best if he entered the building and further investigated."

"A sound decision," the man said, nodding his approval. "Agent Ali, what were the results?"

"Unfortunately, before I could enter said building, the Americans arrived, four of them," Abdul said. "All of them were dressed as natives, in thawbs and abayas. We believed them to be on a mission similar to our own."

"The rescue of Miss Nahar?"

"Yes, sir."

"Proceed."

Abdul clasped his hands and a rueful expression crossed his face. "All I could think was *those damn Americans are bollixing up our assignment again.* So Agent Spencer and I decided to wait and see what they were up to. We believed that they were also conducting surveillance. We did not expect them to actually make a rescue attempt. Especially so quickly. We believed we still had some time to snatch Nahar on our own."

"I see." The man took a sip from a dainty porcelain teacup.

"I don't think you do, sir," Tillie said. "Instead of conducting surveillance, all hell broke loose. The bloody Americans launched an offensive right then and there."

The man's eyes narrowed. "How so?"

"One of the agents, whom Agent Ali identified as his niece, Hope Ali, came barreling out of the building with several armed men in pursuit. Soon two other men, who appeared to be neighborhood slackers, took up the chase. And then another man, obviously some sort of a government operative stashed in a café across the way."

"Bloody brilliant, I must say," the man said. "A nice piece of distraction." He nodded at Tillie. "Go on."

"A few moments later, a car drove up, and two of the agents hustled Nahar into it and took off. She appeared to be drugged, sir."

The man sighed and took another sip from the porcelain cup. "And you followed? Both of you followed?"

Abdul nodded. "We thought it best, sir."

"And no one pursued Agent Ali to determine what her role was?"

"No, sir," Abdul responded. "It was pretty obvious to us that her sole purpose was to distract Nahar's watchers. On reflection, her similarity in appearance and size to Nahar most definitely worked in their favor. However, we did not perceive her role to be anything but a distraction. Besides, we had been led to believe that she would remain otherwise engaged."

The man frowned. "How so?"

"Well, sir, I'm sure you are aware that there is a price on my brother Harun's head. My niece would be of value to the right people, those who could use her as leverage."

"*Bloody hell!* What did you do?"

Tillie flushed. "After Abdul identified her, we simply alerted one of our contacts, who sent a backchannel message to Abdul's nephew that she was in country. It is well known Khalid had issued a BOLO for his sister and would pay handsomely for information pertaining to any sighting. We simply allowed our contact to benefit financially, and we hoped to benefit as well. We thought Khalid would be able to raise enough of a stink to convince the authorities to detain Hope at the airport, thus creating a distraction we could use to snatch Nahar for ourselves. We encouraged our contact to suggest that."

The man cocked an eyebrow.

Abdul cleared his throat. "You know how bloody emotional the Americans are, sir. Once the authorities had Agent Ali, they would drop everything to bail her out. That's what they do." He sniffed. "They have this *leave no man behind* mindset. They value agents over mission. We thought the car holding Nahar would turn around and make a rescue attempt before leaving the city, thereby giving us another shot at Nahar. We were wrong."

"What *did* happen when you arrived at the airport?"

Tillie shook her head. "Unfortunately, the Americans proved a little too crafty. They managed to evade us. We wound up snarled in traffic. It was a very unfortunate situation. We arrived at the airport a little too late."

"So, they bested you, eh?"

Abdul nodded. "Admittedly, the Bentley we procured from the Embassy was an inappropriate choice for vehicular pursuit, sir. It is a bit of a clumsy ox. Unwieldy in the UAE's narrow snickets."

The man frowned. "You did not consider that in advance?"

Tillie frowned. "We selected a vehicle that would blend in while conducting surveillance, sir. We did not expect interference from the Americans. Indeed, we were not aware that they had more than a passing interest. If we had anticipated the need to pursue them, I assure you, we would have selected something more suitable."

"So, you lost them? Your pursuit was for naught?"

Abdul winced. "Yes, sir. Once we lost them, we headed to the airport, assuming that after they picked up my niece, that would be their destination. But they were gone. There was no sign of an American plane anywhere at the Fujairah airport." He frowned.

"Perhaps they went by land or to another airport? Abu Dhabi or Dubai?" Tillie began to play with the hem of her jacket, distressed. "They were obviously much better prepared than we anticipated."

"That's because they had two planes. One commandeered by the U.N. The other owned by a Sheikh from Oman. They made a clean getaway. Unfortunately, their Agent Ali did not."

Tillie gasped. "What do you mean?"

"She was beaten within an inch of her life by an angry mob. A mob incited by her brother, Khalid. He recruited the religion police and was able to get them in place rather quickly."

Tillie frowned. "I thought they were disbanded."

The man snorted. "Groups like that never disband, they just step back and strike when no one's looking."

Abdul nodded. "They are everywhere in the Middle East. Even though they are no longer officially sanctioned in many countries, they still go after women for inappropriate dress or couples for overt displays of affection. Since most still find those activities offensive, their intervention is welcomed." He paused. "You have to understand. They fear they are losing their culture to corrupt influences. The younger people have embraced the Western World. Its influence has been invasive. Teenagers no longer respect the dictates of their fathers. Instead, they leave home in acceptable attire and change at school, stuffing their abayas and thawbs in their backpacks. They put their traditional dress back on before heading home. It's not uncommon for a member of the religion police to follow them and report to their parents. If those parents respect Islamic tradition, those children are punished. Sometimes, severely."

"So, they went after Hope Ali?" Tillie asked.

"Apparently, somewhere along the way, she shed traditional dress and continued on wearing some sort of skintight bodysuit that was quite revealing. Encouraged by Khalid, they decided to punish her. She was kicked, stoned, and beaten."

Tillie gasped. "Wait a minute, he was there? We thought he was home, in Saudi Arabia."

"Apparently not. Either he was already in the UAE or he is capable of teleporting, like our Dr. Who."

Tillie shook her head. "That was not the plan—wait a minute. Did she survive?"

The man nodded. "Barely. Her pickup was waiting nearby. They were able to intervene. They managed to get her out of there, but my understanding is that she is in serious condition, just upgraded from critical. Her injuries are severe. It will take some time before she can return to duty. Clearly, the Americans believe you were involved. That's why they have requested the interview. If they manage to verify your involvement, it would not surprise me if"—he pointed at Tillie—"she came for you. They have nicknamed her *Wonder Woman*. Apparently she is a very skilled agent. I would watch your back. *Both of you* should watch your backs. She is not without resources. She is more than capable of exacting revenge.

"In fact, it might be wise for you two to lay low for a while. Get out of the country. Take an extended vacation."

Tom pushed Hope's wheelchair into the meeting room. Her foot was in a boot and her wrist in a soft cast, but the bruises on her face had faded into an almost unnoticeable yellow. Unfortunately, the clothing she wore hid more bruises, cuts, scars, and stitches, included the scar in her belly button from the incision made during surgery to sew up tears to her stomach lining and liver

Hope's gaze swept the other faces gathered around her. Each of the people present had been the victim of a violent assault. Although they had survived, they suffered from various forms of trauma, including Post Traumatic Stress Disorder, or PTSD. Some appeared to be whole, their bodies intact. Others, like Hope, were still recovering from their injuries. But all of them were broken inside.

Tom tapped her shoulder and whispered into her ear, "I'll be back in an hour." Hope grabbed his hand and held it tight. He kissed her cheek. "You can do this, sweetheart. Be strong." He turned and left the room.

The group leader, a middle-aged woman with bobbed blonde hair graced with discreet purple stripes, nodded at Hope and smiled. "Good, we're all here," she said. "My name is Ellen. I am the staff psychotherapist at this esteemed facility. For those of you who are first-timers, this is the Trauma Group. The place where you can safely yell, scream, cry, and pout about injuries sustained in the line of duty. Each and every one of you has been tossed a shit sandwich. You have been shot, tortured, beaten or suffered some other egregious harms—something few have experienced and even fewer understand.

"Let me be clear. You *will* have nightmares. Your brain is still processing your trauma, so nightmares are expected. We will teach you and your loved ones how to deal with them. Eventually, they will fade.

"You will also find that certain things in daily civilian life trigger a negative response—a noise, a word, an object. Your response may be panic, fear, anger, tears, or violence. We want to discover those triggers here, so you can learn to anticipate and deal with them. Do not be ashamed of them. They are part of who you are now. There is strength in admitting they exist and embracing them. They do not control you. *You* control them.

"Some of you lost friends in the incident that brought you here, others were alone. That you survived is a testament not only to your strength and our quality medical care but also to divine intervention." Ellen smiled. "You survived for a reason and that will eventually become clear to you.

"In the next twelve weeks, we will be meeting two days a week. I will also be consulting with each of you individually as needed. I am here for you twenty-four hours a day during your stay. You can call me anytime, night or day. I don't care if it's six in the morning or eleven at night. If you need me, call me. I may be groggy when I answer, but I wake up easily. I will be able to listen.

"My hope is to guide you through the grieving process. There are five steps—denial, anger, depression, compromise, and finally, acceptance. As individuals, you will experience each of these stages differently, but we will discuss each one as you pass through it. If you get stuck on any step, you must talk about it. Your recovery depends on it."

Ellen smiled at the group. "Please know that I do not take what happened to any of you lightly. There is no way to prepare anyone for the trauma you experienced. All we can do is give you the tools to deal with it after it happens." She nodded at Hope. "Hope, this is your first time here. Why don't you begin?"

Hope opened her mouth to speak, then quickly closed it. *Come on, girl, you can do this.* Again, she tried to speak, but tears welled up in her eyes and she emitted a sob. Hope gazed at Ellen. *Why do I feel so helpless?*

Ellen smiled at her, her expression kind. "It's okay, Hope. Each and every one of us understands your pain. Take your time. Just tell us what you're feeling."

Hope nodded and tried again. "My name is Hope," she began softly. "Three weeks ago, I was severely beaten by a group of religious fanatics, an attack . . ." Her voice faltered. Hope swiped at the tears that trailed down her cheek. She straightened in her chair and said angrily, "An attack that was organized by my brother. Goddammit, my own brother wanted me dead." She sobbed, and a strangled sound emerged from her throat. "My fucking brother watched as a mob kicked me and beat me and pelted me with stones. I almost died, and he did nothing."

Ellen stood and walked to her. She gently placed a hand on Hope's shoulder. "How does that make you feel, Hope?" she asked.

Hope shook her head. "Pissed, angry, confused, betrayed." She closed her eyes and said, "I have always been confident of my ability to keep myself safe, out of harm's way. I have been well trained. I thought I could survive anything." She sobbed again. "Now, I just feel devastated. I cry myself to sleep, my boyfriend thinks I'm loony tunes, my parents want me to quit my job and come home . . ."

Ellen began to massage her shoulder and said, "You're safe here, Hope. Get it out. Let us help you heal."

"Heal? How the fuck am I supposed to heal?"

"One day at a time, Hope. You may feel broken now, you

may believe your life is in pieces. But your Agency leaves no one behind. They are determined to help you pick up the pieces and heal. It's not a matter of if, but when. But you have to want it, Hope. You have to *want* to heal.

"The only decision you have to make now is whether or not you want to heal. Then we'll work on the rest."

Hope gazed at her, the tears running down her face. Finally, she said in a halting voice, "I don't think I can."

Tom sat outside the therapy room and buried his head in his hands. God, these past three weeks had been awful. Smiles from the woman he loved had been far and few between. It was like someone had extinguished the spark within her. Her confidence was gone. She was a mere shell of the Hope Ali everyone had known. In fact, she wasn't Hope at all. He would kill for a giggle, just a mere slip of laughter.

Someone sat down and placed their hand on his. "She's going to be okay, Tom," Cate said. "Somehow, someway, we'll help her find a way through this. I really believe that." She sighed. "Hope went through hell. She thought she was going to die, and she has just started living. That's heady stuff for someone her age. She was snatched from the jaws of death and she doesn't know what to make of it. She needs to find her new normal. and that's not going to be easy."

Tom stared off into the distance. "She thinks it's her fault. She blames herself. I don't know how to help her."

"Well, the transcript of the events leading up to the attack don't bode well for her. She didn't exactly follow orders. In fact, she revealed some of that old impulsiveness. There is no way to know if she would have avoided trouble if she had run straight to her pickup spot, instead of playing around."

"Well, we won't know that until she tells us, will we? And she won't talk about it. She refuses to talk about it."

Cate patted his arm. "She will. When she's ready. Besides, the matter is still under investigation. Remember, she kept repeating her brother's name after she was rescued. She obviously saw him. We're still trying to figure out how he knew she was there. But we *will* figure it out. Dianna and Janet are tracking phones, tapes of conversations culled from satellite surveillance — they are leaving no stone unturned."

Tom shook his head. "I don't know if I can help her get through this. I feel just as broken."

"Tom, we're all in this together, and together, we'll bring her back. She has rarely been alone. Someone has been with her around the clock, comforting her, keeping her connected to life. She knows she's loved. And in the end, that is what will pull her back. Even if she did screw up, she'll learn from it. She's smart. She's feisty. She plays to win. Hope's not broken. She's just trying to find the best way to regain her footing."

Tom sighed. "I hope you're right. Dammit, I *know* you're right." He gazed at Cate. In a choked voice, he asked, "What if she moves forward without me? What if I remind her too much of the past? One she no longer wants to remember?"

"Tom, you're the first person she asked for when she woke up. Yours is the hand she clings to when she gets scared. You are the person she reaches for when she needs comfort. You are her center, her rock. If anything, she's afraid that if she did screw up, you might love her less. She needs to know you are there for her, no matter what.

"She hurts in a million little ways, Tom. Help her heal."

EPILOGUE

Tillie dropped onto the lounge chair and slowly laid her head against a firm pillow.

She adjusted her lime-green polka-dotted bikini, pulled her *Jackie-O* sunglasses over her eyes, and took a sip of her bottled Perrier. Her gaze swept the pool area. She was alone for now. *Thank God.* The last thing she needed was screaming brats splashing in the pool, while their shrieking mothers attempted to herd them.

Tillie closed her eyes. She had come to Paradise Island to relax, unwind, and recharge. "This sure beats London in winter," she murmured to herself. "I so deserve this."

Tillie had taken her superior's warning to heart, immediately leaving the UK for a three month's leave. She had wandered through Europe for a while, but when the weather started to turn, she had hopped on a jet and come to the Bahamas. She was checked in under an assumed name. She had paid for everything in cash, so there was no paper trail if the Americans were actually looking for one. Tillie was quite confident she could not be found. She had effectively gone underground.

Given the number of people on the island, she was careful to keep a low profile. For two weeks, she had remained in her room, ordering room service while catching up on movies and books. On her rare excursions to one of the resort's pools, she had carefully studied those around her. No one had seemed interested in her at all. If there were any watchers, they were good. *Very good.*

Tillie reached down and patted her bag. If anyone did attempt to intercept her, she was well prepared. Her beach bag not only contained her gun, but also other weapons, such as an exploding compact, a lipstick tube that sprayed a paralytic, and her favorite, a deck of cards with edges so sharp they inflicted a thousand cuts with the flick of a wrist. She smirked. She was quite sure she had seen that particular trick in some old movie.

As the sun warmed her body, Tillie's muscles relaxed. *Ah, life was good.* After she closed her eyes for just a few minutes, she would take a dip, maybe swim over to that quaint pool pub, and indulge in an American favorite, the Margarita. Make a toast to her colonial pals. Tillie sighed happily, then she drifted off into sleep.

Tillie was jarred awake when she heard someone settle onto the chair beside her. She had not intended to sleep so deeply. Still, she had selected a deck chair far away enough away from the pool area. Just her luck that some schmuck would join her. *Maybe if I ignore them, they will go away.*

Keeping her eyes closed, Tillie sniffed audibly and rolled onto her side, away from the intruder. *Probably some old fart hoping to flash some cash and entice me to spend the evening with him.* Then she heard more footsteps and someone sat on the chair on the other side of her. *Damn! Just go away, already!*

"Hello, Tillie," said a familiar voice.

Tillie's eyes shot open, and she sat up so quickly she nearly tipped out of her chair. She struggled to regain her balance and then gazed at the speaker. "Dianna? What in the bloody hell are you doing here?"

"Well, if Muhammed won't come to the mountain, the mountain must come to Muhammed, don't you think?" Dianna grinned.

"Though that doesn't mean we're comparing you to Mohammed, because you hardly qualify," said a woman with a lyrical British accent. Tillie turned her head to the chair on the other side of her. A very young olive-skinned woman with big brown eyes and long brown hair, wearing a barely-there yellow bikini, waved at her. "Hi, I'm Hope. The one you attempted to throw to the wolves in the UAE?" She cackled. "Oh, oh, looks like English is losing her rose. She's as white as a sheet."

An older woman moved her chair closer to them. She wore a bright pink tank suit with bright pink toes to match. The woman pulled her sunglasses down her nose, revealing ice-cold blue eyes. "I'm just here to supervise." The woman smiled sweetly. "Just pretend I'm not here."

Tillie's gaze landed on the woman's beach bag. It was surprisingly full, as if it contained something heavy. *A weapon?*

"Me, too," chirped another woman. "Just here to witness the inevitable." The woman gathered her blonde curls up in a fist and attempted to wrangle them into a messy bun at the top of her head. "Though we've met. At the God's Delight compound, where you were so willingly spreading your legs for Reverend John?" She smirked. "How'd that turn out for you?"

Tillie's eyes narrowed. "You're the Ambassador's daughter." *Shit!*

Cate flopped back onto her chair and made a languid motion with her arm. "That I am." She chuckled. "But the reason I'm here has nothing to do with diplomacy. If I had my way, we'd be burning your ass at tonight's bonfire. Low and slow. Just like a barbecued pig."

The other women snickered.

Alarmed, Tillie slowly slid her right arm toward her beach bag. She didn't know what these women wanted but she —"

"Looking for this?" Hope flashed Tillie's gun at her. "One of my many, many skills. If you had a pocket in that gaudy two-piece, I'd tell you to check that, too. Because it would be empty." She chortled. "Things do tend to disappear when I'm around." She blew on her hand. "Magic fingers." She pulled out Tillie's other weapons. "Oh look, antique spy toys." Hope smirked. "Ours are much smaller and much more efficient." A wicked expression crossed her face and she clapped her hands, causing Tillie to jump. "Boom! You're dead."

Tillie's gaze darted from woman to woman. Finally, she said, "Well, this is quite the hen party. How nice of you all to stop by for tea."

Dianna snorted. "See? That is exactly why the British are so warped. All those tea leaves rotting your brain and your teeth."

Tillie glared at her and huffed. "As if."

The unknown blonde woman shook her head. "Girls, girls, girls. Play nice." She pointed at Tillie. "Now, this is how it's is going to go. You've put all three of these women in danger because of your reckless, narcissistic behavior. Two of them almost died. So, you're going to sit here like a good little MISix agent and listen to what they have say." Her eyes narrowed. "You will answer their questions or suffer the consequences. And we're not talking a time-out here."

Hope giggled. "God, Janet, you sound like my mom."

Janet laughed. "Too bad she couldn't make this coffee klatch. She'd be brutal." Her smile was a bit malevolent. "I am much nicer." She flipped her blonde hair over her shoulder. "Well, most of the time."

Tillie deliberately rolled her eyes. "Why are you here? I'm on a well-deserved vacation and I would like to get back to it. This little *mean girls* act does not intimidate me."

Dianna laid back on the lounge chair. She picked up a pink drink with an umbrella attached and took a long sip. "Oh, relax. We just want to clear the air."

Tillie sighed. "Go ahead, then. Let's get this over with."

"Well, first of all, you owe me an apology," Dianna said.

"For poisoning me. I mean, who does that? I was undercover and you tried to take me out. Why?"

Tillie scowled. "It was a mistake. Look, I was protecting you. Making you sick kept Reverend John away from you. That man was a perv, and he enjoyed forcing women to do whatever he wanted. You have no idea what kind of crap that guy was into. How he deliberately tried to warp The Chosen's thinking."

The Chosen was a group of women that Reverend John, the leader of the cult, God's Delight, had recruited to not only run his operation but also cater to his sexual needs. Tillie had been a member — an active member.

Tillie gazed directly at Dianna. "You would have become his sex slave, and he had some very cruel ways to ensure your cooperation."

"I almost died." Dianna glared at her.

"And I'm sorry for that. I just wanted to make you sick. To keep him away from you. How was I supposed to know you were allergic to *Caapi*? Besides, I thought they would ship you out as soon as you fell ill, but Reverend John refused. He got paranoid. Thought the Americans would come down on him or something."

Cate nodded. "That part is true. I tried to convince him to let me take you home, so you could get proper medical care. He outright refused. In fact, he was downright unreasonable about it. Still, that doesn't excuse —"

Tillie held up a hand. "However, I also didn't know you were some sort of secret agent. I just thought Bennie was a nickname. I only discovered that you were actually a spy after I returned home."

Dianna scrunched her nose, her disbelief apparent. "And you didn't think it a bit odd that someone you knew showed up at God's Delight? That someone who had been kidnapped and sold by the same slave trafficking cartel suddenly appeared on your doorstep? Oh, come on. I am calling you on your bullshit. That has *obvious* written all over it."

Dianna took another sip of her drink and said disdainfully, "I spent most of my time worrying you were going to expose me. You had a good thing going down there. You were treated like a princess. Had regular sex with a man who appeared to be a stud." She smirked. "He did seem to be packing. But I digress . . .

"You also had power over a whole bunch of human slaves, all of whom were controlled with a mind-altering drug. You never had it so good." Dianna's eyes narrowed. "You were protecting yourself and your new status in life, no one else. Admit it."

Tillie felt her anger rising. "That is so untrue. I am an agent of the United Kingdom. I was there to determine whether Reverend John was an integral part of the heroin pipeline into the UK. Once I discovered that his interests were much broader, I stayed. I believed the lives of British citizens were at risk."

Cate hooted. "And your superiors bought that? Shit. I had sex with the guy, too. He was good, but he was also a pig. I had to keep myself from shuddering in disgust every time he touched me." She stared at Tillie. "I was also on assignment. I had only been there a week, but I could not wait to get out of there. You were hooked on Reverend John, no question. That was obvious."

"What about turning my brother on me in the UAE?" Hope asked. Her glare was glacial. "Khalid wanted me dead, and you wrote that ticket."

"How did you reach that conclusion?" Tillie shifted in her chair, forcing a bored expression onto her face.

"Well, we followed the trail from one Agent TS Six Nine Zero Five One to Mehdi Azar to Khalid Ali." Janet smiled. "It was a bit tedious, but Dianna and I managed to piece things together. You should have been more careful about using an unsecured cell phone in the UAE. Our satellite surveillance is kick ass. Plug in a day, approximate time, and location, and we can pin down most anything. So we know you were in contact, even if through a third party. Tell us, dear sweet Tillie. What did you do?"

Hope began to impatiently tap her foot. She moved close to Tillie. Her angry stance indicated she was ready to strike.

"Look, I didn't know he was in town. I thought he was in Saudi Arabia. I just wanted to make some trouble. Create a distraction at the airport so we could nab Nahar. I thought he'd arrange to have you detained or something. I didn't know he intended to harm you. Seriously, how could I know that?"

Slowly, Janet said, "One broken rib, a lacerated liver, a torn stomach muscle, a broken wrist, a seriously sprained ankle, multiple lacerations, a black eye, a head wound, pelvic and back bruising. Twelve weeks in intensive psychotherapy. If you had done your homework, you would have known he intended Hope harm. A man doesn't put out a BOLO out on someone because he wants to send her chocolates. If Cate hadn't had medical training, we might have lost her on the plane. And if we had, you would be dead. The entire Agency would have been gunning for you."

Tillie glared directly at the woman. "Seems you got what you wanted. You got Nahar." She frowned. "Though, come to think of it, there has been nothing in the news, so maybe you don't have her." Tillie sat up straighter. "Is that why you're really here? Because you lost her?"

Hope laughed. "Right. Like what happened to me was all in vain. We've got Nahar and the book. In fact, my parents were charged with reviewing her book, and my mother is addressing the U.N. Security Council at this very moment, filling them in on the details, including a little British slip-up.

You know, the one where you tried to make nice with ISIS and few others? Bulloxed that, didn't you? Interesting how a few weapons traced back to the Brits wound up in the wrong hands."

"I know nothing about that," Tillie snapped.

"Oh, then why *were* you after Nahar?" Janet asked, her tone nonchalant. "Issuing an invitation for tea?"

Tillie blushed. "No, we were concerned for her safety. Is she safe?"

Janet nodded. "She's in the wind, in our witness protection program. You'll never find her. And as for her book, you'll receive a heavily redacted version, in a year or two. Nahar has been paid handsomely for her book by the United States government. We *own* it." She cocked her head. "Do you even consider the collateral damage when you engage in your hare-brained schemes? You're a loose cannon, Ms. Spencer. Someone needs to rein you in. Or shut you down."

Tillie attempted to hide her discomfort. Had she really been so caught up in winning that her actions hurt others? No, she was just very committed to her job. Her actions were solely intended to get the job done. Sure, she made mistakes. But they were mistakes, accidents. How was she to know that others would be hurt? She closed her eyes and took a deep breath. "Okay. I get your point. People were hurt, but that was never my intention. And I don't know what I can do to prevent it in the future. I can't prevent what I can't predict. That's impossible. It's not like you share your plans. I can't help it if we get in each other's way."

She stared at the four women before her. "Besides, you know how it is. In our world, women have to try harder. Be better. We have to think outside the box. Sometimes, we have to take chances that men don't."

Hope, Janet, Dianna, and Cate groaned.

"Damn, I can't believe you fell back on that horseshit line,"

Hope said.

Tillie gazed at Hope. In a belligerent tone, she declared, "Look, I'm sorry. I really *am* sorry, but I did what I thought best. My conscience is clear. Besides, you don't appear to have any lasting damage."

Hope snorted. "You keep telling yourself that. Hell, I've got scars in places most people will never see. Not only was I crushed physically, but I was also crushed mentally. I fell down that deep dark rabbit hole and almost didn't crawl back out. Because *you* did what you thought best." She shook her head. "God save me from self-righteous, overly ambitious bitches. Until Janet and Dianna discovered otherwise, I was beating *myself* up over what happened. I thought I had brought all of this down on myself."

Janet interjected, "Sure, Hope is young and strong. But she's also human. You almost succeeded in destroying her confidence. And we didn't know if she'd get it back."

Hope's voice broke. "You almost tanked my career. *Bitch.*"

Janet held up a hand. "However, we all learned something, and that's what matters." She nodded at Dianna.

"Look, we don't trust you, but we do have an offer for you," Dianna said. "We're building a new team. We think you could be an asset. And frankly, we feel the need to keep you close. So you don't throw us under the bus again."

Tillie's eyes widened. "Leave MISix? Are you nuts?"

Dianna laughed. "Not even. You couldn't begin to qualify for our Agency. We're an elite crop of lawyers who pursue justice where others can't. Technically, we don't even exist. Hell, we're funded under environmental services in the national budget." She shook her head. "No, MISix has agreed to loan you to us for certain projects." She smirked. "As some sort of consolation prize for interfering with our operations in the past. Interpol and some of the other European intelligence agencies have agreed to loan us operatives as well. But your boss said the final decision is up to you."

"You hate me. Wouldn't your negative attitude have an impact on our relationship? On my ability to get the job done?"

Dianna flapped her hand at Tillie. "We *can* work together. We just won't be best buddies. However, you need to be aware that your actions have had negative consequences. We don't hold grudges, but we do want to keep the collateral damage to a minimum. Maybe if we worked together and communicated more, we could all win."

"Well, you Americans *have* been a pain in my ass . . ."

"Ditto," Cate snarked. "A real big pain . . ."

"Girls," Janet said in a warning tone. "Retract the claws."

Hope nodded. "That shit gets us nowhere. If we can't work together, then we go our separate ways." She grinned.

"And may the best woman win."

YOU MAY ALSO ENJOY THE FOLLOWING FROM EXTASY BOOKS INC:

The President's Daughter
Seelie Kay

Excerpt

Sarah hurried into the coffee shop and threw herself into the booth currently occupied by her friend, Lisa Barzak. She smiled at her and looked around. "What? No Mike? I thought you two were attached at the hip."

Lisa swatted at her. "Oh, very funny. Mike's in Hollywood, doing final edits for his new movie. It's scheduled for release on Christmas Day, but I don't think it's going to make it. That's only four weeks away. I just hope he makes it back in time for Christmas."

Sarah smiled. "You think he's finally going to pop the question?"

Lisa laughed. "It's only been nine months, but he has been complaining about my P.I. work. Thinks it's too dangerous. So if he wants me to cut back or take a desk job, he's going to have to put a ring on it." She waved her left hand and wiggled her fingers.

Lisa had met Milwaukee native Mike Reardon, star of the Hard Man movies, the prior year. A living, breathing action hero, Mike Reardon was a force to be reckoned with at the box office and in real life. He had his finger in almost every major Milwaukee children's charity, spreading largesse from an apparently bottomless bank account. He was the local boy who made good.

Lisa, on the other hand, had left the local police force after earning her paralegal certificate. She now worked for her cousin, Casey, a general practice attorney, as a paralegal and a private investigator. Although most of her cases involved surveilling unfaithful spouses or people faking injuries to claim disability, she sometimes got involved in sticky situations. Mike had freaked out when she had been accosted by a gunman after a checking out a building that turned out to be a warehouse for illegal weapons. Although Lisa had managed to disarm the gunman, the incident had pushed Mike to declare his intentions.

Sarah sighed. "Well, it's probably just as well. I'm not sure I want anyone else to hear what you've found. I feel stupid pursuing this. I mean, if the guy is a relative, wouldn't I have known about it by now? Wouldn't someone have been looking for me?"

Lisa pulled out a large brown envelope and started pulling out paperwork. She sighed. "Maybe not. Because if he was looking, there wouldn't have been much to find. What I found is disturbing, and I think, worthy of further investigation."

Sarah pulled at her hair and frowned. "Seriously?"

Lisa placed two certificates on the table. She pointed at the one bearing Sarah's name. "I think the birth certificate you gave me is a fake. I couldn't find any record of your birth in Iron Mountain, MI, nor Dickinson County. In addition, the certificate says you were born at Hamilton Hospital. There has never been any such hospital in Iron Mountain. I also found no record of a Sarah Lee Pearson being born anywhere in Iron Mountain or Michigan. I checked the entire year prior and after your birthday. Nothing. Then I did a nationwide search with your birthdate. I found eight females born on that day at approximately the same time. None with your name."

"That makes no sense—"

Lisa held up her hand to silence Sarah. "So, I did a little more digging. Of those eight, six are still alive, one has died, and one was listed as missing." She pointed at the other birth certificate. "Sally Jane Powell. Born the same day, same time, also at Hamilton Hospital, but in Albany, New York. Hamilton is a private birthing hospital for wealthy people. Now, look at the names of the parents, Sarah. Anna and Jamisen."

Sarah paled. "The Senator's daughter?"

Lisa nodded. She pulled a newspaper clipping from her envelope. "Sally was taken from her home at age five, allegedly by her nanny, Mary Engelton. There was a nationwide manhunt. Neither she nor the nanny were ever found. It is considered a cold case."

"You think I'm Sally Jane Powell?"

"I can't confirm that, not without a DNA test, but . . ."

About the Author

Seelie Kay writes about lawyers in love, with a dash of kink.

Writing under a nom de plume, the former lawyer and journalist draws her stories from more than 30 years in the legal world. Seelie's wicked pen has resulted in fourteen works of fiction, including the Kinky Briefs series, The Feisty Lawyers series, The Garage Dweller, A Touchdown to Remember, The President's Wife, The President's Daughter, and Seizing Hope, as well as the romance anthology, Pieces of Us.

When not spinning her kinky tales, Seelie ghostwrites non-fiction for lawyers and other professionals. Currently, she resides in a bucolic exurb outside Milwaukee, WI, where she shares a home with her son and enjoys opera, the Green Bay Packers, gourmet cooking, organic gardening, and an occasional bottle of red wine.

Seelie is an MS warrior and ruthlessly battles the disease on a daily basis. Her message to those diagnosed with MS: Never give up. You define MS, it does not define you!

Seelie can be reached at www.seeliekay.com, www.seeliekay.blogspot.com, or on Twitter or Facebook.

www.ingramcontent.com/pod-product-compliance
Lightning Source LLC
Chambersburg PA
CBHW060618130626
46555CB00002B/553